The
CODE BUSTERS
Club

CASE #6

The Secret of the
Puzzle Box

Penny Warner

MINNEAPOLIS

*To Yuka Hayashi, the inspiration for the
new Code Buster, Mika*

Darby Creek
A division of Lerner Publishing Group, Inc.
241 First Avenue North
Minneapolis, MN 55401 USA

For reading levels and more information, look up this title at www.lernerbooks.com.

Cover art by Victor Rivas.
Interior illustrations © Laura Westlund/Independent Picture Service.

Main body text set in Gazette LH Roman 12/21. Typeface provided by Adobe Systems.

Library of Congress Cataloging-in-Publication Data

The Cataloging-in-Publication Data for *The Secret of the Puzzle Box* is on file at the
Library of Congress.
ISBN 978-1-5124-0307-7 (trade hardcover)
ISBN 978-1-5124-0900-0 (EB pdf)

Manufactured in the United States of America
1 – SB – 7/15/16

CODE BUSTERS CLUB RULES

Motto
To solve puzzles, codes, and mysteries and keep the Code Busters Club secret!

Secret Sign
*Interlocking index fingers
(American Sign Language sign for "friend")*

Secret Password
Day of the week, said backward

Secret Meeting Place
Code Busters Club Clubhouse

Code Busters Club Dossiers

IDENTITY: Quinn Kee

Code Name: "Lock&Key"

Description
Hair: Black, spiky
Eyes: Brown
Other: Sunglasses

Special Skill: Video games, Computers, Guitar

Message Center: Doghouse

Career Plan: CIA cryptographer
or Game designer

Code Specialties: Military code,
Computer codes

IDENTITY: MariaElena—M.E.—Esperanto

Code Name: "Em-me"

Description
Hair: Long, brown
Eyes: Brown
Other: Fab clothes

Special Skill: Handwriting analysis, Fashionista

Message Center: Flower box

Career Plan: FBI handwriting analyst or Veterinarian

Code Specialties: Spanish, I.M., Text messaging

IDENTITY: Luke LaVeau

Code Name: "Kuel-Dude"

Description
Hair: Black, curly
Eyes: Dark brown
Other: Saints cap

Special Skill: Extreme sports, Skateboard, Crosswords

Message Center: Under step

Career Plan: Pro skater, Stuntman, Race car driver

Code Specialties: Word puzzles, Skater slang

IDENTITY: Dakota—Cody—Jones

Code Name: "CodeRed"

Description
Hair: Red, curly
Eyes: Green
Other: Freckles

Special Skill: Languages,
Reading faces and body language

Message Center: Tree knothole

Career Plan: Interpreter for UN or deaf people

Code Specialties: Sign language,
Braille, Morse code, Police codes

CONTENTS

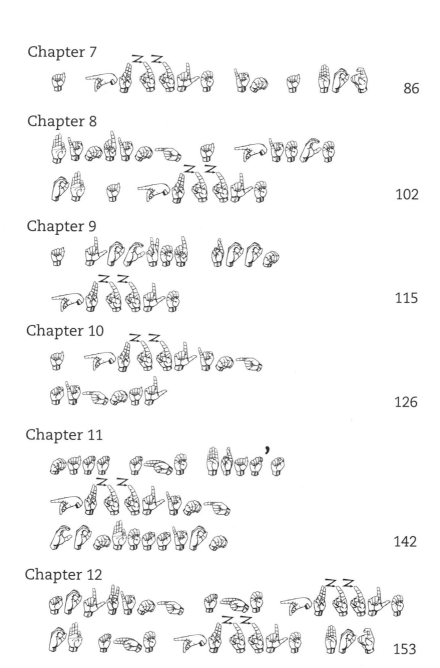
To crack the chapter title code, check out the CODE BUSTERS' Key Book & Solutions on page 167, 173.

READER

*To crack the chapter title code,
check out the Code Busters Key Book
& Solutions on pp. 167 and 173

To see complete Code Busters Club
Rules and Dossiers, and solve
more puzzles and mysteries, go to
www.CodeBustersClub.com

Chapter 1

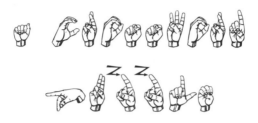

F erry to the shore,
Scavenge for some hidden finds,
Snap, but do not take . . .

On her way to school Monday morning, Cody Jones recited the poem aloud to her friend MariaElena Esperanto (M.E. for short). Their teacher, Ms. Stadelhofer, had given them a haiku— a Japanese-style poem—that offered a clue about their next field trip. Cody had read it so many times that she had it memorized. But she still wasn't sure what it meant.

"Any ideas?" she asked M.E., hoping her friend had figured it out over the weekend.

"Shore, scavenge, snap," M.E. mused. "Maybe we're going to the shores of Hawaii to scavenge for snapping turtles."

Cody rolled her eyes. "I wish!" she said. The sixth graders at Berkeley Cooperative Middle School had already taken one long-distance field trip: a super-fun visit to Washington, DC, where they'd gone to the International Spy Museum. Cody, M.E., and the other Code Busters—Quinn Kee; Luke LaVeau; and their newest member, Mika Takeda—were happy to return home with their souvenir disguises and memories of the adventure. On the plane trip back from the East Coast, Cody and M.E.'s teacher, Ms. Stadelhofer, hinted that the students would be going on another field trip in a few weeks. Cody couldn't wait to find out what their next destination would be.

She'd just have to wait for Ms. Stad to explain the poem to the class. Still, she couldn't help wondering what new adventures, mysteries, and codes were waiting for them.

"Welcome back to the classroom, students!" Ms. Stad announced after the final bell rang and the students were settled in their seats. "I hope you all enjoyed the trip to our nation's capital. I thought it was wonderful, in spite of the little mishap that occurred."

Ms. Stad looked directly at Matt Jeffreys, who squirmed in his chair under her all-knowing eye. Matt's antics had almost ruined the trip.

"For your homework, you all received a secret message, written as a haiku," Ms. Stad began. "Do you remember what a haiku is?"

A few hands went up, including Mika's. Mika and her family had recently moved to California from Japan. At first, she'd been too shy to raise her hand, but she'd come out of her shell during the trip to Washington, DC.

"It's a Japanese poem that has five syllables—or beats—in the first line, seven in the second, and five in the third," Mika said when Ms. Stad called on her.

"Haikus are usually written about nature, but they can be about anything."

"Correct!" Ms. Stad said, looking pleased. "Now, does anyone know what *this* haiku is about?" She recited the poem for the class and then glanced around the room.

Cole's hand went up cautiously. "Maybe it's about a boat ride?"

"Why do you think that, Cole?" Ms. Stad asked.

"Because it says 'ferry to the shore.' Are we going on a ferry?"

"Yes, that's part of it," Ms. Stad said. "Very good. But there's more."

Lyla, in the back row, raised her hand. "The second line says 'scavenge for hidden finds.' I think we're going on a scavenger hunt!"

"You're right!" Ms. Stad said with excitement in her voice.

"Awesome!" Matt the Brat called out without raising his hand. "Are we going to look for buried treasure?"

Ms. Stad frowned at Matt's outburst, then raised

an eyebrow and said, "You'll see. Now, what about the last line? 'Snap, but do not take.' Anyone?"

Matt spoke up again without raising his hand. "Oh, snap!" he said, laughing.

"Matthew," Ms. Stad warned, "please raise your hand if you want to be called on."

He shrank back in his seat.

Ms. Stad called on the boy across from Cody. "Francesco, do you know what the last line means?"

"Uh, snap, like a tree branch?" Francesco guessed.

"Good guess, but no." Ms. Stad shook her head and then called on Bradley.

"Like something broken?" Bradley said.

"Nope," Ms. Stad said. "Try again."

Matt the Brat raised his hand and then said without waiting to be called on, "It's too hard! Just tell us!"

"Take a moment to think about it," Ms. Stad told Matt and the class. Cody tried to think. What do you snap? A finger? A rubber band? A photo . . .

That had to be it! Her hand shot up.

Ms. Stad called on her. "Cody?"

"Snap could mean snapshot, like taking a picture."

"Exactly!" Ms. Stad said.

"And maybe 'do not take' means we'll be taking *pictures* on the scavenger hunt instead of actually taking *things*," Cody continued.

"Absolutely correct!" Ms. Stad announced.

"But we still don't know where we're going," Stella said.

"It's probably someplace related to what we're studying," guessed Mika.

"I bet it's the Amazon River," Grace guessed.

"Or Atlantis!" Stephanie said.

"There's no such place as Atlantis," Tessa told her. "That's a myth."

"Are we going back to Alcatraz?" asked Francesco.

"Whoa!" Ms. Stad said, waving her arms. "One at a time. And please raise your hands if you have something to say. Actually, though, I'm not going to tell you exactly where we're going. You'll get to figure it out for yourselves."

Ms. Stad picked up a stack of papers from her desk and began passing them out to the rows of students. Cody looked at her copy and grinned. It was a crossword puzzle! She and the Code Busters loved crossword puzzles. They were just like coded messages. Luke was always making up crosswords for the others to solve.

After everyone had a copy of the puzzle, Ms. Stad explained the assignment. "In the haiku I gave you, there were clues about where we're going on our next field trip and what we'll be doing. But you'll have to solve the crossword puzzle to find out exactly where we'll be. When you're finished with the puzzle, turn your paper over and don't tell anyone else. You may begin now."

They got to work.

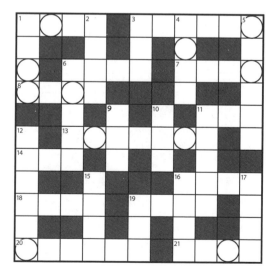

Each question was written in alphanumeric code, which substitutes numbers for letters of the alphabet, such as "1" for "A," "2" for "B," "3" for "C," and so on. Underneath was a list of words that matched the questions. *Easy*, thought Cody. *After you solve the code, all you have to do is match the right word with the question.*

Cody pulled out her alphanumeric decoder card and went over each question. She filled in the answers using the numbers as a guide.

Across

23-8-1-20 1 4-5-20-5-3-20-9-22-5 14-5-5-4-19

23-8-5-14 19-15-13-5-20-8-9-14-7 9-19 21-14-4-9-19-3-15-22-5-18-5-4

  6. 1 2-12-1-3-11 2-9-18-4

  7. 23-8-1-20 1 2-9-18-4 8-1-19

  8. 5-12-5-3-20-18-9-3 6-9-19-8

  11. 3-8-5-23 1-14-4 19-23-1-12-12-15-23

  13. 15-21-20-4-15-15-18 15-22-5-18-14-9-7-8-20

  14. 1 13-9-7-8-20-25 20-18-5-5

  16. 9-14-19-5-3-20-19 20-8-1-20 2-21-26-26

  18. 1 16-1-12-9-14-4-18-15-13-5 15-6 20-15-15-20

  19. 20-18-5-5-19 8-1-22-5 20-8-9-19

  20. 12-15-15-11 6-15-18 3-12-21-5-19

  21. 23-8-1-20 23-5-12-12 2-5 20-1-11-9-14-7

Down

1. 23-8-1-20 19-16-9-5-19 21-19-5
2. 12-9-19-20-5-14 23-9-20-8 20-8-5-19-5
3. 23-8-15, 23-8-1-20, 23-8-5-14, 23-8-5-18-5, 23-8-25, 1-14-4
4. 1-12-19-15 3-1-12-12-5-4 19-21-14-18-9-19-5
5. 23-8-5-14 25-15-21 19-12-5-5-16
6. 21-19-5 20-15 20-5-12-12 20-9-13-5
9. 1 20-1-12-12 6-21-26-26-25 1-21-19-20-18-1-12-9-1-14 2-9-18-4
10. 2-18-5-1-20-8 20-8-9-19
11. 1 20-1-12-12 23-8-9-20-5 2-9-18-4
12. 23-8-1-20 1 18-1-9-14-2-15-23 8-1-19
15. 19-5-5 20-8-5 19-9-20-5-19
16. 15-21-18 18-9-4-5 20-15 15-21-18 4-5-19-20-9-14-1-20-9-15-14
17. 20-8-5 9-13-13-9-7-18-1-14-20-19 18-9-4-5 20-15 20-8-5-9-18 4-5-19-20-9-14-1-20-9-15-14
18. 7-9-22-5 1 3-8-5-5-18!

Code Busters Key and Solution found on pp. 167 and 173–174.

It didn't take Cody long to translate the alphanumeric code and then match the answers to the questions. But she still didn't know the answer to the big puzzle—the class's field trip destination. Disappointed, she turned her paper over and waited for the other students to finish.

Eventually Ms. Stad called "Time!" All the kids put down their pencils. "Turn your papers over and check your answers as I read them," Ms. Stad directed the group.

As Ms. Stad reviewed the correct answers, Cody checked off each one. She'd gotten them all right.

"Does anyone notice something different about some of the crossword squares?" Ms. Stad asked.

Milan raised his hand. "Some of the squares have circles in them."

"Right!" Ms. Stad said. "Now, at the bottom of your paper, write down all the letters that are in the circled squares. You should have eleven letters."

Cody did as directed, writing down the *L* in the first word, the *N* in the second word, and so on, until she had this:

LNADGELANSI

Cody stared at the message. All she had was a bunch of random letters that still didn't mean anything. She glanced around at the students sitting nearby. Everyone else looked puzzled too. She wondered if such a long series of letters could be an anagram—a word with all the letters scrambled up.

"What's LNADGELANSI supposed to mean?" asked Matt without raising his hand. "I never heard of that place."

"It means," Ms. Stad replied, "that you're not finished solving the puzzle."

Cody raised her hand. "Ms. Stad, is this an anagram?"

Ms. Stad looked delighted. "Yes, it is! Who besides Cody remembers what an anagram is?"

M.E.'s hand shot up. "It's when you take a word and mix up all the letters and put them in a different order."

"Correct," Ms. Stad said. "Only this time there are *two* words mixed together to make it even more of a challenge. See if you can figure out what two words the letters spell. Then you'll know where we're going on our trip."

Cody wished Luke were there to help her. He was really good at anagrams. In fact, he wrote a lot of his secret messages in anagrams. Cody studied the letters to see if any words jumped out at her.

SALE. LID. LASS. GLIDE. LEND.

Next, she tried some common letter combinations, such as "ing."

DING, SING, SLEDING.

That didn't work. Finally, she thought about the clues in the poem and in the crossword to see if they made sense together. *Boat, ferry, shore*—that could mean . . .

She checked off the letters. Yes! It had to be *island*!

That left ALEGN. She tried GALEN. LEGAN. ELGAN. NAGLE. AN . . .

And then she got it! She knew where they were going on their next field trip!

Just then M.E. passed a note to Cody. Cody unfolded the origami paper and read the words M.E. had translated into Spanish: *Isla de los angeles*!

Chapter 2

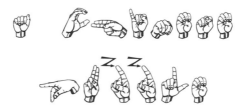

Cody had heard of Angel Island, but she'd never been there. Before Ms. Stad could explain more, Matt the Brat blurted out, "What's Angel Island?"

Ms. Stad smiled patiently. "Angel Island is a small island in the San Francisco Bay that's rich in California history."

"Does it have prisoners like Alcatraz?" Matt asked. The class had visited Alcatraz on a previous field trip.

"No, and you won't find the ghosts of Al Capone and Diamond Dave on Angel Island, either," Ms. Stad said.

"Bor-ing," Matt muttered as he slouched down in his chair.

Ms. Stad ignored him. "But like Alcatraz, it's also a state park. And we're going to camp there overnight, along with Mr. Pike's class!"

Cheers went up from the students. Cody remembered the last time the two classes had gone camping at the Carmel Mission. The Code Busters had discovered a hidden map and a coded journal that sent them on an unexpected adventure. Maybe they'd find something equally exciting this time.

"Over the years," Ms. Stad continued, "the island has been a hunting ground for the Miwok Indians, a stopping point for Spanish ships, a Civil War military fort, a transport station for World War II troops, a quarantine inspection hospital, an immigration station for Asian and European immigrants, and a detention facility for prisoners of war. It was even a storage site for missiles during the Cold

War, but the military closed that site in 1979. When we tour the place, you'll still be able to see the missile launchpad."

American Indians and European explorers? Cody thought. *A hospital and immigration station? A prison and a military base?* That was a lot for a small island! She wondered why people had been quarantined there. Did they have some terrible disease?

"If there's no missiles anymore, why are we going?" Matt asked, tapping his pencil. He could never just sit still.

"We're going to Angel Island to find out more about our heritage," Ms. Stad said. "People of many different backgrounds spent time there. Since we have a diverse group of students whose families come from various places around the world, we're going to learn about where your ancestors came from and how they came to call this land home. I've written a list of two-letter country codes, like AF for Afghanistan and AU for Australia, and put them in Morse code, since it's a universal code. See if you can crack these codes and match them with the countries they stand for. When you're done, circle the country codes that are connected to your heritage."

Country Codes

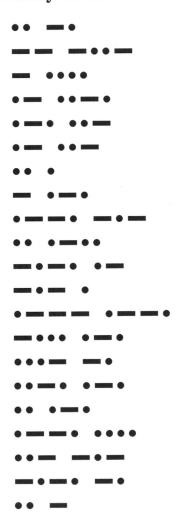

Countries

Afghanistan	Japan
Australia	Kenya
Brazil	Mexico
Canada	Pakistan
China	Philippines
France	Russia
India	Thailand
Iran	Turkey
Ireland	United Kingdom
Israel	Vietnam
Italy	

Code Busters Key and Solution found on pp. 167 and 175.

Cody went to work translating the Morse code list into country abbreviations, using her Morse code decoder card. She soon had all the codes deciphered and started matching them to their countries. Though she got stuck on a few, eventually she figured out each pairing. Then she circled the two countries that applied to her background—Ireland and the United Kingdom.

Once all the students were finished, Ms. Stad continued. "Remember how we've been talking about where our ancestors lived before they immigrated to the United States to find a better life? Many of them either landed at the Angel Island Immigration Station on the West Coast or came through Ellis Island on the East Coast. We're going to be studying genealogy and creating family trees, so Mr. Pike and I thought you'd enjoy visiting the place where some of your relatives might have landed when they first arrived."

Francesco's hand shot up. "My great-great-grandparents came from Italy and went through Ellis Island. I saw their names in a big book when we visited New York last year. They had to stay there three days because my great-great-grandmother was sick and they wouldn't let them leave until she was better. They almost got sent back to Italy."

"That happened a lot, Francesco," Ms. Stad said. "The immigration department was very strict about who they let into our country. A person had to be healthy, with no criminal record, and have a place to live and work. If they didn't meet those requirements, they were either turned back or they had to stay on the island, sometimes for weeks or even years."

Wow, Cody thought. It was sad to think that a family could come all the way to America hoping for a better life and then end up in jail or have to turn back.

"I'm adopted," Jodie said. "I don't know where my birth parents are from."

Ms. Stad was about to say something when Matt interrupted again.

"Mine are from New Jersey," he shouted out.

Ms. Stad shook her head. "Matthew, your ancestors may have ended up in New Jersey, but they had to come from somewhere before that."

"Well, they came from Italy like Francesco's," Matt said. "One of them was a real actual pirate."

"Yeah, right," said Liam in the back.

Matt turned around and glared at him. "It's true. His name was Vincenzo Gambi, and he was a pirate with Jean Lafitte in New Orleans."

Ordinarily, Cody would've assumed Matt was just making up stories for attention. But those names sounded pretty specific—not like something Matt would come up with on his own. Maybe he was telling the truth.

"That's interesting, Matthew," Ms. Stad, her eyebrow raised. "Uh, anyone else? M.E.?"

"My background is American Indian and Mexican," M.E. answered. "Everyone on my mom's side is from Mexico, and my relatives on my dad's side are Cherokee. I'm the only real American here!"

"We're all real Americans," Ms. Stad said. "But we all have different ancestry. Some people call the United States a melting pot, but I prefer to think of it as a salad bowl. We all live and play and work together, but we still keep parts of our own backgrounds and cultures."

"If we're a salad, I wanna be the big tomato," Matt said in an Italian accent.

Ms. Stad eyed him. "Matthew."

Matt tucked his head down. He began drawing furiously on the paper in front of him.

Ms. Stad continued. "We'll begin preparing for our expedition to Angel Island by creating our family trees."

She began passing out papers to the students. Cody took hers from Matt and saw that it was blank.

"I'd like you to draw the trunk of the tree at the bottom of your paper and label it with your name." Ms. Stad demonstrated on the board by drawing a trunk and adding the words "Ms. Stadelhofer" at the bottom. "Next, draw two branches, one on either side, and write down the names of your parents." She showed them what to do. "Then above each of their names, draw two more branches and write the names of your grandparents on both sides. Stop when you've finished that much."

The students began their drawings, following Ms. Stad's suggestions. Matt turned around in his seat and glanced at Cody's picture of a tree trunk.

"That looks more like a volcano," he said, grinning.

"Matt, you're being rude," Ms. Stad said. "Turn around and do your own work."

"Rude is my 'tude, dude," Matt whispered to Cody before he obeyed the teacher's command. Cody shook her head and returned her attention to creating her family tree.

After drawing a trunk at the bottom, she carefully wrote her full name inside: *Dakota Jones*. Underneath she added her younger sister's name, Montana. Neither of the girls had a middle name. Her mother said it was a family tradition.

Next, she drew a branch on the right side of the trunk and wrote her mother's name: "Susan O'Gara." She drew another branch on the other side and wrote her father's name: "Matthew Scott Jones."

Cody had met all her grandparents, although she didn't see them much anymore, since they still lived up north in the California Gold Country. Her mother's parents—Nana and Papa—were named Colleen and Casey O'Gara. She knew their ancestors were Irish, but she didn't know much more than that. On her dad's side were Pop-Pop and Grammie—also known as Matthew and Mary Jones. They came from a Scottish background, but she was clueless about anything more.

Cody glanced over at M.E.'s tree. It was already filling up. Cody wondered how M.E. would fit all her aunts and uncles and cousins on the tree. She had a big family.

When the students were done with their tree trunks and lower branches, Ms. Stad said, "All right, everyone, here's your homework for tonight. First, find out the names of the *next* generation of your ancestors—your *great*-grandparents—if you can."

Cody thought that part would be easy. All she had to do was ask her parents about their grandparents.

Ms. Stad started passing out another paper. "Next," Ms. Stad continued, "use your decoder cards to decipher the International Alphabet Flag Code on the homework sheet, and follow the instructions once you've cracked the code."

Cody recognized the flag code immediately. The Code Busters often used it to send secret messages. Each flag stood for a different letter of the alphabet. It would take a few minutes to decipher, but it wouldn't be hard.

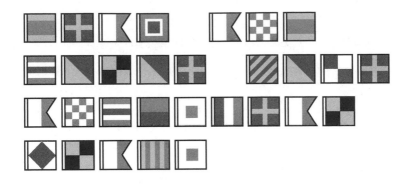

Code Busters Key and Solution found on pp. 168 and 176.

"And finally," Ms. Stad said, "remember I told you that many of Angel Island's immigrants were kept for a long period of time at the immigration station? Well, some of the Chinese immigrants scratched out poems on the walls while they waited to be released. There's a copy of one of the poems on your homework paper. Isla, would you please read the poem aloud?"

Isla sat up straight, took a breath, and began to read:

Waiting, watching clouds above, the sky darkens.
Now the moon fades behind the billowing fog.
Freedom flies just out of reach, leaving sadness.
Soon, despair fills the heart and the clouds cry.

24

"Thank you, Isla," Ms. Stad said. "That poem was written by a Chinese immigrant while he was on Angel Island, waiting to enter the United States. These kinds of poems are often written to fit inside a square, with each line exactly the same length. For your homework, I'd like each of you to write a poem about how it would feel to stay for a long time at Angel Island, not knowing when, or if, you would ever be allowed into this country. This time, instead of a haiku, please write your poem in the style of the Chinese poem. The next poem on your paper explains the assignment. MariaElena, would you please read that poem?"

M.E. smiled at being called on and began to read:

In the first line, express the idea.
For the second, expand on that thought.
With the third line, add something new.
Then in the fourth line, tie everything together.

"Thank you, MariaElena," Ms. Stad said. "Students, that second poem tells you how to write your own poem."

Cody had already begun thinking about what she'd say in her poem, but Ms. Stad wasn't finished.

"One more thing, class. Many of the poems that the Chinese immigrants wrote on the walls at Angel Island had hidden messages within them. See if you can figure out the secret message in the first poem we read."

Cool, Cody thought. A message hidden in a poem. But would she be able to solve it?

Chapter 3

After school, Cody, M.E., and Mika headed up the hill to the Code Busters Clubhouse hidden in Berkeley's eucalyptus forest. The girls were on their way to meet the other two Code Buster members, Luke and Quinn, and find out if the boys had the same mysterious homework assignment.

When the girls arrived at the clubhouse, made out of old billboards and covered with a camouflage parachute, Cody gave the secret knock—her initials in Morse code:

Code Busters Key and Solution found on pp. 167 and 176.

Then she called out the password, "Yadnom"—the day of the week said backward. The girls waited for the door to unlock and open. A moment later, they were greeted by Quinn and Luke.

"Were you followed?" Quinn asked, peering outside to look for strangers, lurkers, or spies.

"No," Cody answered, although she couldn't be sure. Matt the Brat often tailed them when they headed for the clubhouse. "At least, I didn't see anyone."

"No mountain lions either," M.E. added, then shivered. The Code Busters had already had one close encounter with the wild animal. While M.E. loved animals, she was always on the alert for the more dangerous ones.

"Good," Quinn said, as the girls entered. "Did you hear about Friday's field trip?"

The girls removed their backpacks and sat down cross-legged on the carpeted floor that covered their hidden stash of code-busting supplies. Luke was keying in something on this cell phone, and Cody wondered what was up.

"Yeah, we're going to Angel Island!" M.E. said. "Did you guys get the same homework assignment?" She showed Luke and Quinn the paper Ms. Stad had given them.

"Yep, same one from Mr. Pike," Quinn said. "Luke's looking up some of the country codes we're stuck on."

"Got them!" Luke announced, glancing up from his phone. "IE stands for Ireland, and IN is India." He and Quinn filled in the answers on their homework papers.

"We got all of those," Cody said, "but we can't figure out the Chinese poem. It's supposed to have a hidden message in it."

"Oh yeah," said Luke. "Mr. Pike said when the poem was written in Chinese, the characters lined up to form a square."

"That's what Ms. Stad said too," Cody replied. "But I tried lining up all the words and they came out uneven." She showed them the work she'd done on another sheet of paper.

Waiting, watching clouds above, the sky darkens
Now, the moon fades behind the billowing fog
Freedom flies just out of reach leaving sadness
Soon, despair fills the heart and the clouds cry

"See? The first line has seven words, the second and third lines have eight words, and the last line has nine words. They don't make a square. And even when I squish all the words and letters together, it's still uneven." She showed them the back of the paper with the jagged right edge.

Waitingwatchingcloudsabovetheskydarkens.
Nowthemoonfadesbehindthebillowingfog.
Freedomfliesjustoutofreachleavingsadness.
Soondespairfillstheheartandthecloudscry.

Mika nodded. "Yeah, but the problem is, I bet it only forms a square when you use Chinese characters, not English words."

"Right!" said Quinn, smiling at her. "I'm taking a Chinese class on Saturdays, and I'm learning to write in Mandarin. This poem would look totally different in its native language."

"So can you translate the poem back into Chinese characters?" asked Cody eagerly.

Quinn shook his head. "I'm not that fluent. But I don't think we need to do that. I think we're looking at this the wrong way."

"How are we supposed to look at it?" M.E. asked.

Quinn held up his paper. "Well, the only words that line up evenly in the English version are the first words of each line. See?"

"Yeah, so?" M.E. said, squinting at the poem. "That's how most poems are written."

"True," Quinn said, "so read the words in the poem that *do* line up perfectly."

Cody studied the poem a moment, running her finger down the first words on the left-hand side. "Cool!" she said, finally seeing what Quinn meant.

M.E. shook her head, frowning. "I still don't get it. Mika, do you see it?"

Mika stared at the paper. Then her face lit up. "Yes!" She turned to M.E. "Here. Read the *first* words in each line."

M.E. said the four words aloud. Her eyes widened. "You think that's the hidden message?"

"It has to be," Mika said. "Since the poem was written at the Angel Island immigration station, those four words together make perfect sense."

M.E. read the four words aloud again, pausing after the first comma. "It sounds so sad," she said.

Mika shook her head. "I think it sounds hopeful."

The kids were quiet for a few moments as they thought about the hidden message of sadness and hopefulness. Cody pulled out a sheet of paper, suddenly inspired to create her own poem about what it would be like to be stuck on Angel Island after a long voyage. Using Ms. Stad's instructions, she began writing two lines about being on the island; a third line that added something new; and finally, a line that tied everything together. The others followed her lead, but Cody was done first.

A Poem about Angel Island
by Cody Jones

Away from my country, adrift at sea,
Hoping for a new life and home.
I'm not welcome at this place.
Living, and waiting, between two worlds.

When she was finished, she read the poem to the other Code Busters, who were working on their own poems.

"Not bad," Luke said, giving it a thumbs-up.

"Yeah," M.E. added. "You're awesome at writing poems."

Cody shrugged. "But there's no hidden message in it."

"Yes, there is," Mika said. "Read the first words from each line—*away, hoping, I'm, living*. That says it all!"

Cody grinned. "I guess that works."

After half an hour or so, all five kids had finished their Chinese-style poems, complete with hidden messages. It wasn't easy, but Cody thought that adding a message made the poem more fun.

"What's the next part of the assignment?" M.E. asked.

"We're supposed to find out more about our heritage," Cody said. "I know my grandparents' families are from Ireland and the United Kingdom, and that some of my ancestors came to America because there was a big famine. I'll have to ask my mom and dad to tell me more when I get home."

"Me too," M.E. said. "I'm part Mexican and part Cherokee, but I don't know exactly where my relatives came from or how long they've lived in this area."

"Mine are all from Japan," Mika said. "Actually, my great-great-grandparents came here a long time ago and were at Angel Island before they moved to San Francisco."

"No way!" said Cody. "Why didn't you mention that in class?"

Mika shrugged. "Well, it seemed like a lot of people wanted to talk about their ancestors. There wasn't time for everyone to share a story."

Typical Mika, thought Cody. Unlike Matt, who always wanted to be the center of attention, Mika was good at listening to others.

"But if your great-great-grandparents immigrated here, how come you weren't born here?" asked M.E.

Mika explained, "After they died, their son—my great-grandfather—moved back to Japan. Most of my relatives still live in Tokyo. That's where my parents and I lived until my dad got a job here. I'm curious about what the immigration station was like, since my ancestors were actually there."

"Same for me," said Quinn. "I think some of my relatives may have stayed on Angel Island for a while too. My mom has a big book full of stuff about our family. I know my great-great-grandfather was born in the Guangdong Province of southern China, and I've heard stories about my great-grandparents coming to the United States because they were so poor. But now I'm excited to find out more."

Luke shrugged. "I don't know much about my family. My *grand-mere* took me in when my parents died. She's Creole, from Louisiana—part French, part Spanish, part African. She said some of our relatives also came from Haiti. She doesn't talk about them much because they're hard to track down. I think if you go back far enough, a lot of our ancestors were slaves."

The kids were quiet for a moment. Cody couldn't imagine what it must have been like when slavery was legal in so many places, including the United States. She wondered if there was a way the Code Busters could help Luke find out more about his family background.

"We'd better get to work on drawing our country flags," Mika said, breaking the silence. "They're due tomorrow."

The Code Busters got out fresh sheets of white paper, plus their colored markers. They drew flags based on their heritage and colored them in.

Cody's flag had three vertical stripes—green, white, and orange—representing Ireland. Mika drew a white flag with a red circle in the middle for Japan. Quinn's flag for China was red with yellow stars in the corner. M.E. drew the flag of Mexico, which had green, white, and red stripes, plus a coat of arms in the middle—a picture of an eagle with a cactus and a snake. Since Luke didn't know what part of Africa his ancestors might have originally come from, he decided to draw the flag of Haiti—blue on top and red on the bottom, with a white stripe and a coat of arms in the center.

When they were finished, they packed their backpacks and headed outside, locking the door to the clubhouse behind them. They were about to head down the hill when something flapping in the wind caught Cody's eye. She looked up to see a flash of color. On a branch of one of the trees that held up the sides of the clubhouse, someone had tied a flag. It had three vertical stripes: one green, one white, and one red.

"Hey, M.E.!" she called to her friend. "Did you put that flag up there?"

The kids turned around to see the green, white, and red flag waving in the air.

"No," M.E. said. "That's not my flag."

"It looks like yours," Cody said.

"No, the Mexican flag has a coat of arms in the middle of it. That one is plain."

"What country is it from?" Mika asked.

Luke got out his cell phone and looked it up. "That's the flag of Italy."

"So who put it there?" Quinn asked, staring up at it.

"Look!" Luke said, pointing down the hill. Just a few feet away was a small paper flag attached to a twig that was stuck in the ground. The flag was red, with a V shape cut into the right side.

"I know that flag. It's on one of our decoder cards," Luke said. He dug into his backpack and pulled out the International Alphabet Flag Code card. "That's the letter *B*."

"Look there," Cody said, pointing down the path. "Another one." This time the flag was blue on the top half and red on the bottom half.

"That's an *E*," Luke called out. "I think someone's sending us a message!"

The kids began following the flags down the hill, reading off each letter. M.E. took notes along the way. When they reached the bottom of the eucalyptus forest, she read the message aloud, stumbling on a few words that were misspelled.

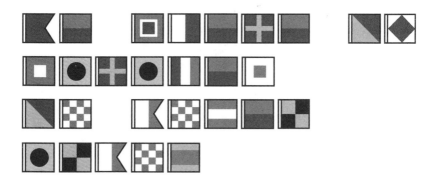

Code Busters Key and Solution found on pp. 168 and 176.

"So who's trying to scare us with that stupid message?" M.E. asked.

Cody crossed her arms. "I think I know," she said, remembering Ms. Stad's discussion about where everyone was from. "Someone in our class said his relatives were from Italy. I'll bet that the same person left the Italian flag at our clubhouse and made those flag messages."

"Matt the Brat!" they all said at once.

Chapter 4

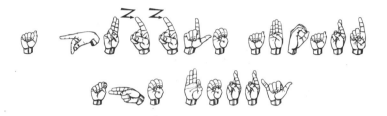

O n Friday, the day of the trip, the Code Busters were beyond excited. They'd spent the past few days digging into their family backgrounds and learning about their ancestors. It turned out that six kids in Cody's class, including Mika, had relatives who'd passed through Angel Island before settling in California. Cody's family didn't have any connection to the island, but that didn't stop her from looking forward to the day's adventures.

At the Berkeley Marina, the students from Mr.

Pike's and Ms. Stad's classes lined up for the Angel Island Ferry, all carrying backpacks loaded with their camping gear. Cody wasn't surprised to see Matt the Brat show up wearing an eye patch, carrying a plastic sword, and sporting a fake tattoo of a Jolly Roger pirate flag. Ms. Stad confiscated the sword, made him put the eye patch in his pocket, and just shook her head at the tattoo.

After everyone was aboard the ferry, the teachers passed out maps of Angel Island, plus a new puzzle for the students to solve. This one was written in semaphore code, often used at sea by sailors. The hidden message was supposed to give the students their first clue for their scavenger hunt on the island. The kids broke up into groups, and the Code Busters met at the bow of the boat so they could solve the puzzle together.

Code Busters Key and Solution found on pp. 168 and 176.

By the time the Code Busters cracked the code, they were even more excited about the trip.

"I wonder where we're going first," Quinn said, looking at the map of Angel Island. "I mean, besides camp and the visitor's center."

ferry pier

China Cove

Immigration Station (North Garrison)

hospital

immigration barracks

mess hall

Ayala Bay

N

Visitor's Center

US Coast Guard (off limits)

ANGEL ISLAND

Fort McDowell (East Garrison)

Camp Reynolds (West Garrison)

Nike missile site X

Perles Beach

to Alcatraz Island

US Coast Guard (off limits)

"Maybe the military base," Luke suggested, pointing to the West Garrison at Camp Reynolds.

"Or the hospital," M.E. said.

"Maybe we'll get to fish at the cove," Quinn said, referring to Ayala Cove, their arrival point.

"I hope it's the immigration station," Mika said, after finding it on the map. "I talked to my grandmother last night and found out more about my great-great-grandfather, Hiraku Takeda, and his wife, Yuka. They were actually there for six weeks before they could leave the island. And the whole time they weren't allowed to see each other."

"How sad," Cody said. "Why couldn't they be together?"

"My grandmother said men and women were kept in separate areas and the doors were locked, so they couldn't even visit," Mika explained.

"Wow, that's awful," M.E. said. "I would hate to be away from either of my parents for that long."

Mika nodded. "My grandmother said Hiraku and Yuka would put tiny secret gifts and messages for each other in little boxes, called Koyosegi puzzle boxes. Then they'd hide the boxes in different places around the island so they wouldn't be found by the guards. With each box, there'd also be a clue about where the next box would be hidden."

"That's so romantic!" M.E. sighed. "I wonder where all their hiding places were."

"My grandmother told me some of them," Mika said. "And she said that Hiraku hid one puzzle box so well that Yuka never found it. After they got off the island and were together again, they obviously couldn't go back for it. So it might still be there!"

"Wow!" said Cody. "Maybe we'll find it."

"I hope so," said Mika. "Hiraku was also a poet. He wrote a lot of poetry under a pen name—Senjin. So maybe he left some poetry behind too, like the Chinese poems we've studied."

"How cool would it be if we could track down something of his?" Quinn said excitedly. "We'll have to keep our eyes peeled."

After a ten-minute ride, the ferry pulled up to Ayala Cove. Cody noticed a flashing light coming from high up the hill and pointed it out to the others.

"What is it?" M.E. asked.

"It looks like Morse code," Quinn said, squinting at the light that continued to flash on and off.

"Is it a flashlight?" Mika asked.

"Looks like it," Quinn said, squinting at the light.

"Can you read the message?" Mika asked.

Quinn studied the pattern and began to call out the letters. M.E. wrote them down as fast as she could.

Code Busters Key and Solution found on pp. 167 and 176.

"Weird," M.E. said, after the light stopped blinking. "What do you think it means?"

Quinn shrugged. "And who sent it? And who's it for? Someone on the ferry?"

Cody immediately thought of Matt the Brat, but there was no way someone on the island would be sending him a Morse code message. She glanced around and noticed another ferry passenger staring out at the island. He had a big tattoo of a pirate flag on his arm, much like Matt's, except this one looked real. The guy caught her watching him and quickly disappeared inside the cabin.

Before she could think more about it, the teachers and chaperones escorted the students off the ferry and onto the dock. Cody glanced up at the rising hill where the light had come from, but the light was gone. She looked back at the ferry, but the man with the tattoo was nowhere in sight.

"This place is so cool!" M.E. said, checking out the landing area. "It's like being in the countryside."

Cody nodded as she looked around. It was a beautiful place, dotted with tall trees, surrounded by blue water, and home to all sorts of wildlife. But there was a loneliness about the place that made her feel a little homesick. The island was so quiet, so far away from the activity of the mainland. She couldn't imagine how lonely some of the immigrants must have felt.

"Follow me to the tram, everyone!" Ms. Stad called out.

The kids hoisted their backpacks and headed for

the blue and white tram that was waiting to take them to the campsite on the other side of the island. Cody was glad she'd be sharing a tent with M.E. and Mika. Ms. Stad had allowed all three to be buddies. Quinn and Luke would be together in another tent. At night the Code Busters planned to communicate in the dark using flashlights to send Morse code messages. Remembering what she'd seen from the ferry ride, Cody wondered, briefly, who else on the island knew Morse code . . .

When everyone was seated on the tram, Ms. Stad and Mr. Pike gave the usual lecture about safety, reminding them to stay with their buddies, to listen to the chaperones, and not to leave the camp alone. The island was only five miles all the way around, but the climb to camp was two and a half miles of steep terrain, and with backpacks and supplies, that would have been a lot. Cody was grateful the tram ride made the trek easy. She looked out at the view of the Pacific Ocean and Golden Gate Bridge as the tram made its way past Camp Reynolds and the West Garrison military base. She found it hard to believe this peaceful, natural island was surrounded by busy city life.

Just as she spotted Alcatraz, the notorious prison island also in the middle of the bay, the tram stopped. They'd arrived at camp!

"Where's the bathroom?" Matt called out as he jumped from the tram. "I gotta go!"

"The latrines are right over there." Ms. Stad pointed to a couple of outhouses just beyond the campsite.

"Gross!" Matt said, holding his nose. "I'm not going in there!"

Ms. Stad smiled patiently. "It's there or nowhere."

"Then I'll hold it!" Matt said and stomped off to put up his tent.

Cody, M.E., and Mika looked at one another and giggled. He couldn't hold it until tomorrow morning.

"All right, everyone," Ms. Stad said. "Remember what the coded message said. Pitch your tents, set up camp, and meet at the visitor's center with your sack lunches. And bring jackets. It gets windy on the island."

With the help of the chaperones, the students got busy putting up their tents and storing their gear. They'd been warned to keep all their food in the wooden camp cupboards so the raccoons and other wildlife wouldn't eat everything. Cody stowed the chocolate chip cookies her mother had made for her and closed the latch. When the girls finished setting up camp, they got their lunches and jackets and met up with Quinn and Luke. The Code Busters followed Mr. Pike's group, taking a shortcut down the hill to the visitor's center.

After the last stragglers arrived, including Matt the Brat and a couple of chaperones who brought up the rear, the kids ate their lunches at the picnic tables. Cody watched the fishermen on the docks, the seagulls overhead, and the boats out on the bay as she nibbled at her peanut butter and jelly sandwich. Then Ms. Stad and Mr. Pike handed out their next scavenger hunt clue.

Cody looked at the paper. At the top, she recognized the familiar symbols of pigpen code. But below that, the page was filled with small drawings.

This didn't look like any of the codes or puzzles she'd seen before.

Ms. Stad began to explain. "Students, your first clue is written in pigpen code. Decode it to learn your first destination. And the rest of the puzzle is written in symbols used by many American Indian peoples. Figure out what these symbols mean using the chart we're passing out now. On the way to your first destination, take snapshots of the five clues. Then wait for everyone else when you get there. You may begin the scavenger hunt!"

The Code Busters gathered in a circle to work on the message written in pigpen code.

Code Busters Key and Solution found on pp. 169 and 176.

Next, the kids went to work on the American Indian symbols.

Code Busters Key and Solution found on pp. 170 and 176.

"Okay," said Quinn when they'd finished, "we have to find and take pictures of these five things, so keep an eye out."

"This should be easy," M.E. said. They began their hike back up the hill toward Camp Reynolds, with their chaperone trailing behind them.

It wasn't long before Luke spotted a bird sitting on a tree limb and took a picture with his phone. Next, Quinn pointed to the mountain range ahead of them and snapped a picture. They had to hike a bit before they found running water in a small creek, and they didn't see a fence until they were nearly to the West Garrison.

"That's four down!" said Luke.

"But we're still missing the animal tracks," Mika added.

Instead of looking around them as they had been doing, the kids focused on the ground, searching for animal tracks. Mika checked her phone for a list of wildlife they might find on the island. "There aren't any squirrels, rabbits, foxes, skunks, opossums, or coyotes on Angel Island. Only deer, raccoons, birds, and rodents."

"Rodents?" M.E. said, scrunching her nose. "You mean, like, rats?"

Cody shivered. She didn't want to think about a bunch of rats running around the island. They totally creeped her out. She'd found one the size of a small cat at her last home and hadn't slept well for a week afterward.

Finally, she spotted what looked like animal prints in the dirt. "I think these are raccoon tracks," she said, taking a picture.

"Great!" Quinn said. "Now we have all five. Let's find Ms. Stad."

The Code Busters, along with their chaperone, were the first group to arrive at the destination— Camp Reynolds. They showed their pictures to Ms. Stad and were rewarded with snacks of fruit, cheese and crackers, and bottles of water. "You can explore the area nearby until the others arrive, but don't wander out of sight. We'll meet in half an hour in front of the hospital building."

Tired from the thirty-minute climb, the kids sat down on a short cement wall and enjoyed their snacks. When they were finished, they decided to look around the garrison, which once housed artillery batteries that protected the island from Confederate ships during the Civil War. A few years later, Camp Reynolds was established as an army camp. Back then the camp had a church, bakery, blacksmith, shoemaker, laundry, barber, and trading store.

"Let's go inside the barracks," Luke said, pointing to one of the decrepit buildings that still stood nearby. The kids followed him into the empty barracks and looked around, trying to imagine what it must have been like for the infantrymen to live there so long ago. Cody tried to picture life without computers, cell phones, and the Internet.

"It's creepy in here," M.E. said. "And there's probably rats. Let's go."

Outside, Mika pointed across the road. "Look. A cemetery! Let's check it out and see if there are any famous names."

They walked over to the small, weedy cemetery surrounded by a white picket fence. M.E. brought up the rear. She didn't like creepy places, and cemeteries were definitely creepy. The others started reading off names and dates from the headstones and crosses.

"A lot of these graves are for people who died on Alcatraz," Quinn said. "They have their prisoner numbers on them, plus their names. I wonder why they were buried here instead of on Alcatraz."

"Because Alcatraz is solid rock," Luke said. "That's why they call it the Rock. You can't bury anything in it."

"Whoa! Look at this one," Cody said, pointing

to an old gravestone. "It says *CAPTAIN BLACK—KILLED IN A MUTINY.*"

"This one says *ZEKE MELVIN—DEAD FROM GUNSHOT WOUNDS,*" Quinn added, indicating another stone.

"This person must have drowned," Mika told the others. "It says, *FOUND ON THE BEACH.* That's so sad."

Just as Cody bent down to read another headstone, she heard a crunch behind her. She stood up, the hairs on her neck tingling, and glanced around. She had the oddest feeling someone was watching them. *Probably Matt the Brat*, she thought, although she hadn't seen him since they left the starting point.

The sound came again—this time from behind a tree beyond the fence. Cody grabbed M.E.'s hand. "Did you hear that?" she whispered.

M.E. appeared to be frozen. She barely nodded, but her wide eyes told Cody that her friend had also heard the noise.

"Who's there?" she called out. Quinn, Luke, and Mika hurried over to Cody and M.E.

"What's going on?" Quinn asked, straining to see where Cody was staring so intently.

"I heard something—or someone. It came from out there." Cody pointed to the trees in the distance.

Luke took a couple of steps forward. "I don't see anything—"

Just then a figure darted from behind one of the trees and ran deeper into the thick forest beyond the cemetery.

"There he goes!" M.E. squealed, pointing.

Luke looked as if he might take off running after the lurker, but instead, he shrugged.

"He's gone, whoever he is," he said. "We must have scared him away."

"Do you think it was Matt?" Mika asked, remembering the last time they thought someone had been following them.

"Probably," Luke said. "He's always spying on us."

"Hey," came a voice from the opposite direction. "What are you guys up to?"

Standing just outside the picket fence at the other end of the cemetery was Matt the Brat.

"None of your business," Luke called back.

Meanwhile, Cody frowned and peered at the trees where the lurker had been hiding.

There was no way that lurker could have been Matt the Brat. Not unless Matt could be in two places at the same time.

So who was the figure behind that tree? Why had he been spying on the Code Busters?

And why did he run away?

Chapter 5

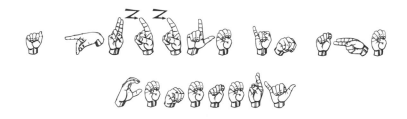

"All aboard!" a grizzled old man in a khaki shirt and pants called loudly. He stood by the tram, gesturing for the students to hop on. "Hurry up, come on, we don't have all day," he said impatiently as the kids filed onto the tram. Ms. Stad and Mr. Pike helped direct the students to their seats, counting them as they stepped aboard.

The Code Busters came running from the cemetery—all but Cody, who lingered a few seconds, trying to figure out where the mysterious figure had gone. Seeing nothing, she quickly caught up with the others and followed them onto the tram.

Ms. Stad stood at the front, frowning. Silently, she counted her students again, put her hands on her hips, and shook her head. "Where's Matthew?"

The kids looked around, but Matt had vanished. "Here we go again," M.E. whispered to Cody. "I hope he doesn't ruin this trip too."

Moments later, Matt came wandering out of the cemetery, holding a long stick as if it were a pirate's sword. He swished it back and forth, fighting invisible enemies as he slowly lumbered toward the waiting tram.

"Matthew Jeffreys!" Ms. Stad said. "You're supposed to stay with your group. Where have you been?"

Matt the Brat shrugged as he stepped aboard. "Nowhere."

"No sticks on the tram!" the driver called out, eyeing Matt in his rearview mirror.

Matt glared at the man and then threw the stick away.

"I'm bored," he said as he headed for an empty seat. "Can't I just go back to camp and read comic books and play video games?"

"No, you may not," Ms. Stad said. "While you're on Angel Island, I'm responsible for you, and I'm not letting you out of my sight again."

Cody looked back at the driver and saw him watching Matt in the mirror. The man's eyebrows were pinched together like one long caterpillar, and his mouth was turned down. Cody wondered if the guy didn't like kids very much or if that was just how his face looked all the time.

"All right, everyone," Ms. Stad began, distracting Cody from the driver's scowl. "We'll be taking the tram all the way to the immigration station. Remember, you're still on your scavenger hunt, so look carefully for coded messages along the way and keep your decoder cards handy. The driver will stop for about ten minutes at each place so you can take pictures."

"Cool," Luke said, pulling out the pack of code cards. "We should be able to ace this."

Quinn nodded. "Yeah, but keep an eye out," he said to the others. "We don't want to miss any of the codes."

"Students," Ms. Stad called out, hushing the excited, buzzing kids. "I'd like to introduce you to our guide for the trip."

For a moment, Cody thought their guide was going to be the crabby tram driver, but instead, a petite young woman she hadn't noticed before stood up from her seat in the front. She turned and faced the students.

Ms. Stad continued, "Everyone, this is Park Ranger Angela Yee. She'll be pointing out the various sites along the way and giving you some history of the island, so I want you to be good listeners." She turned to the woman, who looked very official in her uniform—a brownish-green jacket and slacks—especially with the park ranger badge and various pins that dotted her zippered jacket as if she were an eager Girl Scout. Her black hair was tucked under a peaked, Smokey-Bear-type hat. "Ranger Yee, these are our students from Berkeley Cooperative Middle School."

The kids applauded for Ranger Yee.

"Thank you, everyone," Ranger Yee said into the microphone she held. "Welcome to Angel Island. As your teacher said, I'll be your guide on the tram ride to the immigration station, so if you have any questions, please don't hesitate to ask. Our driver, Delbert Schnikey, will be stopping the tram at some of the sites, but these will be very short stops, so don't wander off. If you miss the tram, it's a long hike up the hill to the next stop."

"Thank goodness we don't have to walk the whole way," M.E. whispered. Cody could tell her friend was already tired after exploring the island all morning.

"As you know," Ranger Yee continued, "the area you just explored is called Camp Reynolds, which was later known as the West Garrison. During the Civil War, artillery batteries were built here to prevent Confederate ships from attacking naval bases."

"Arrg!" Matt the Brat blurted out. "Just like pirates!"

Ms. Stad shot him a look, and he scrunched down in his seat.

The ranger went on with her talk. "The camp later became a place for military recruits. But long before Westerners arrived, the Miwok Indians camped here. They fished; hunted deer and duck; and gathered acorns, roots, and leaves. The island provided everything they needed to live."

"Remember, students," Ms. Stad added, "don't take anything from the park except pictures."

Ranger Yee turned to the driver and said, "All right, Delbert, we're ready to head to the next stop."

Delbert Schnikey grunted and started up the engine. The Code Busters reviewed their decoder cards as they passed oak and bay trees, sagebrush and manzanita bushes, and beautiful wildflowers of all colors. It wasn't long before Ranger Yee asked Mr. Schnikey to stop the tram. Cody couldn't wait to look for a coded message at the site.

"This is Perles Beach," Ranger Yee said, gesturing at the area behind her, which offered a panoramic view of the San Francisco Bay. "In the late 1800s, the navy built fortifications with artillery, rifles, rapid-fire guns, and mortar batteries, all to protect the coast if it was attacked."

"Were there any pirates here?" Matt yelled out. "'Cause my great-great-grandfather was Vincenzo Gambi and he was an awesome pirate. I'm related to him."

Ranger Yee smiled. She looked as if she'd heard the pirate question before.

"Well," she began, "there are rumors that Sir Francis Drake's lost treasure may be somewhere on the island. The English explorer spent a month here in 1579, repairing his ship, the *Golden Hind*. Many people believe that tons of gold, silver, jewels, and other treasures he and his men pirated and plundered from Spanish galleons are buried at his landing point. Unfortunately, no one knows exactly where that landing point was, since Drake's ship log was lost. The treasure could be anywhere, even right here." Ranger Yee swept her arm toward the coastline.

"Anywhere?" Matt said, his eyes wide.

"That's right," Ranger Yee answered. "But so far, no one has found Drake's loot, and it could just be a tall tale that old sailors like to tell."

Cody glanced at Matt, who was staring out at the coast. Did he seriously think there was treasure around here?

"All right, everyone, take a look around, but remember, we'll be leaving in ten minutes."

The kids hopped off the tram and scanned the area for a coded message. Mika was the first of the Code Busters to spot a sign written in flag code, in honor of the Coast Guard.

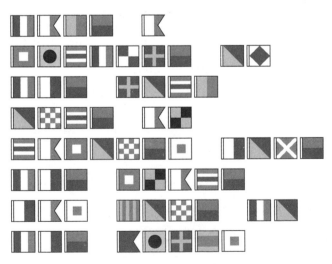

Code Busters Key and Solution found on pp. 168 and 176.

"It's another haiku," M.E. said, writing it down in her notebook.

"This one is obvious," Luke said. "Rock, Al Capone, birds. Duh."

The others nodded as Cody took a picture of the site indicated in the clue. They spent the rest of the time climbing the cement steps and exploring the old battery, where cannons and artillery once stood.

"I wonder what it was like back then," Quinn said. "Too bad there aren't any cannons left. That would be awesome." Quinn loved anything military.

A whistle blew, signaling that it was time to reboard the tram. After everyone was seated and the teachers had finished their head count, Mr. Schnikey started the engine and the tram was off to its next destination.

"Welcome to what was once a Nike missile site," Ranger Yee announced as the tram came to a halt a few minutes later. "It's gone now, removed in 1962, but you can still see where it once was. Beyond it is the US Coast Guard station, but that area is off-limits to the public."

"My uncle was in the Coast Guard," Matt the Brat announced. "He has all kinds of medals and stuff."

Ranger Yee acknowledged Matt with a patient smile before continuing her talk. "Antiaircraft missiles were loaded with TNT and hidden underground, ready to be launched if the country was attacked."

"TNT," Quinn whispered, his eyes wide with interest.

"You're free to look around," Ranger Yee announced, "except for the areas that are off-limits."

Quinn was the first one to spot the coded message underneath a sign that read NO ADMITTANCE. The message was written in phonetic alphabet, a code often used by the military.

**Whiskey hotel oscar sierra echo
mike oscar tango tango oscar   india sierra:
"Hotel oscar november oscar romeo.
Romeo echo sierra papa echo charley tango.
Delta echo victor oscar tango india oscar november
tango oscar   Delta uniform tango yankee?"**

Code Busters Key and Solution found on pp. 171 and 176.

While the others translated the code, Cody glanced back at the tram. Delbert Schnikey was speaking quietly into his two-way radio. He kept glancing over at Ranger Yee, who stood a few feet away talking to Ms. Stad and Mr. Pike. He seemed almost . . . nervous. Or at least as if he was trying to be secretive. Cody wondered who he was talking to. Suddenly Schnikey caught her looking at him and quickly set the radio down.

A moment later, he blasted the tram's whistle and shouted, "Tram's leaving!"

What was that all about? Cody wondered.

Back aboard the tram, she settled in next to M.E.

"What's the matter?" M.E. asked her. "You seem distracted."

Cody avoided looking in the driver's rearview mirror, but she had the sense Mr. Schnikey was watching her. She turned to M.E. and whispered, "Don't look, but I think there's something weird going on with our driver."

M.E. immediately looked at the mirror.

Cody rolled her eyes. "I said *don't* look!"

"Oh my gosh, he was totally looking right at us!"

Cody nodded. "I thought so. Like I said, I think he's up to something, but I don't know what."

"Let's keep an eye on him," M.E. said.

"But keep our distance too," Cody replied. "Just to be safe."

Cody turned her attention to the two teachers who stood at the front of the tram, counting students and making sure no one was left behind. Ms. Stad frowned, her finger tapping the air as she finished her count and started over.

Cody knew that look. Someone was missing. She glanced around and spotted the empty seat.

Matt the Brat wasn't on board.

Not *again* . . .

Chapter 6

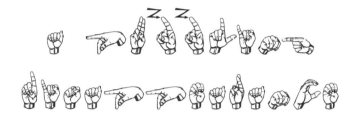

"Matthew!" Ms. Stad and Mr. Pike called out as the students looked on.

"Where could he have gone?" Cody asked M.E. "He was here just a minute ago."

M.E. shrugged. "I don't know, but as usual, he's ruining our trip."

"Should we help find him, like last time?" Quinn asked.

Luke shook his head. "The teachers said to stay here. We'd better not leave."

Cody thought for a moment and then had an idea. "Wait here," she said to M.E. Then she stepped off the tram and headed for Ms. Stad.

"Dakota," her teacher said. "I told you and the other students to remain on the tram. Now go back to your seat. We'll handle this."

"But I think I know where he is," Cody protested. She pointed to the Off-Limits sign that hung on the barbed wire fence.

"Why would he go in there?" Ms. Stad asked. "We told him to stay away from the restricted areas."

Cody shrugged. "He thinks he's a pirate or something. He's probably looking for Drake's lost treasure. I saw him staring out that way when Ranger Yee talked about it."

Ms. Stad sighed and shaded her eyes as she looked toward the fenced area. Cody did the same and spotted someone walking along the coastline. It looked as if he was stabbing the ground with a big stick.

"There he is!" Cody called out. She pointed toward the figure.

"Oh, for goodness' sake!" Ms. Stad mumbled, shaking her head.

Mr. Pike headed over to Matt, who appeared to be digging in the dirt. When the teacher got closer, Matt dropped the stick, hung his head, and slowly followed Mr. Pike back toward the tram.

"What were you thinking, going off like that?" Ms. Stad said when Matt and Mr. Pike reached her.

Matt shrugged and kept his eyes on his dirty sneakers.

"Listen, young man," Mr. Schnikey said. "I don't put up with this kind of nonsense on my tram. You're off the tour."

Ms. Stadelhofer turned to the driver. "Wait a minute, Mr. Schnikey, you can't just leave him here. He's my student and my responsibility."

"Yeah, well, this is *my* tram and *your* student is interfering with *my* job," Schnikey said, jerking a thumb toward Matt. "Like I said, I don't tolerate this kind of behavior. I'm not just the tram driver, you know. I'm in charge of maintenance and security around here. I can't have some kid running wild where he doesn't belong!"

Ms. Stad looked surprised at Schnikey's outburst. She turned to Mr. Pike, who said, "Well, we could send him back to camp with one of the chaperones."

Matt's grim expression suddenly brightened. *Wow,* Cody thought, *he's getting his way after all. This whole time he'd just wanted to go back to camp and read comic books and play Zombies versus Teachers.*

Ms. Stad shook her head. "No, he'll stay right here on the tram. Mrs. Raleigh, will you please sit with Matt and make sure he behaves?" she asked one of the parent volunteers. The woman nodded and moved over to share Matt's seat. "Matthew, if we can't trust you to stay with the group, I can't let you join us on the rest of the stops. You'll have to stay on the tram with Mrs. Raleigh."

Matt made a face and looked away.

The rest of the students settled back into their seats, and the tram ride resumed, with Mr. Schnikey at the helm.

The Code Busters talked in sign language on the short ride to the next stop, so the other students wouldn't know what they were saying.

asked M.E.

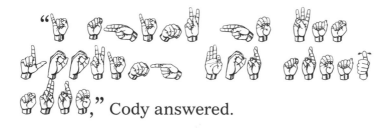

," Cody answered.

Mika offered.

Luke's eyes narrowed.

Cody nodded.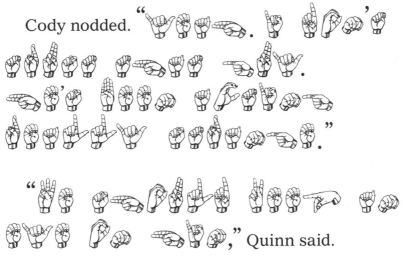

Code Busters Key and Solution found on pp. 171 and 177.

The tram pulled up to their next destination—Fort McDowell at the East Garrison.

As soon as the tram came to a halt, Ranger Yee stood up. "This is where the detention center and discharge camps were built," she announced, continuing her history lesson about the island. "In the late eighteen hundreds, military troops coming back from war were kept here at the hospital if they had any contagious diseases, such as smallpox. The rest were released, or discharged, from service and replaced by new recruits. The fort was closed down after World War II."

"Thank you, Ranger Yee," Ms. Stad said. "Students, we'll be taking a longer break here for snacks and water. After you're finished, you're free to search for the next coded puzzle." She eyed Matt, reminding him silently that he would remain on board.

The students disembarked the tram and collected their snacks. The Code Busters headed for a nearby picnic table, gobbled up their food, tossed their trash in the bins, and then began searching for the next coded message.

Cody was the first to find it—a sign taped to the hospital building marked *E Wing*. "There it is!" she said, pointing it out for the others. The kids ran over and studied the message. This one was written in alphanumeric code, where numbers substituted for letters. Cody got out her decoder card and began translating the message, while Quinn took down the information in his notebook.

24-8-1-20'19 13-9-19-19-9-14-7? 10-15-12-22 13-25
18-9-4-4-12 1-14-4 20-1-11 1 16-9-3-20-21-18.

25-15-21'12-12 6-9-14-4 13-5 . . .

1-20 20-8-5 2-5-7-9-14-14-9-14-7 15-6

  5-20-5-18-14-9-20-25

1-20 20-8-5 5-14-4 15-6 20-9-13-5 1-14-4 19-16-1-3-5

1-20 20-8-5 2-5-7-9-14-14-9-14-7 15-6 5-22-5-18-25

  5-14-4,

1-14-4 1-20 20-8-5 5-14-4 15-6 5-22-5-18-25

  16-12-1-3-5.

Code Busters Key and Solution found on pp. 167 and 177.

"This is hard!" M.E. complained after studying the riddle for a few minutes. "Is it something like air?"

"Or maybe time?" Quinn suggested.

"Or even the universe?" Mika offered.

"It could be something like the middle, because the clues keep repeating *beginning* and *end*, *beginning* and *end*," Cody said.

Luke shook his head. "I think it has something to do with the letters. Did you notice how some of the words in the instructions were misspelled?"

The Code Busters looked at the first deciphered

sentence and then Quinn said, "They're all missing the same letter!"

"That's it!" M.E. exclaimed, after reading the riddle aloud again. "We were looking at it in the wrong way. We were trying to find an object, when all the time it was a letter."

"So we're supposed to take a picture of it?" M.E. asked. "There must be billions of them around here."

Luke pointed to the hospital building. The letter they were looking for was right in front of them. "That has to be it," he said.

He took a picture of the letter displayed on the side of the hospital building. The kids spent the rest of the time exploring the area before it was time to return to the tram. As they began heading back, Cody noticed Mr. Schnikey standing off in the trees. He appeared to be talking to someone, but Cody couldn't see who it was.

"Is that one of the chaperones he's talking to?" Cody asked the others, nodding in Mr. Schnikey's direction.

"I don't think so," Quinn said. "But it sure looks like he's up to something."

Mr. Schnikey was gesturing to the other person—a man. Schnikey looked angry, but then again, the tram driver always seemed to be mad about something. He pulled something out of his pocket, glanced around as if to make sure no one was looking, and passed it to the other guy. The mystery man took the object, put it in his pocket, and pulled out something from his other pocket.

Cody tapped her right fist against her left palm, the ASL sign for "money."

"Ooks-lay ike-lay *ots-lay* of-yay oney-may!" Quinn whispered in Pig Latin as he stared at the two men.

Code Busters Solution found on p. 177.

Luke frowned. "Yeah, that's weird," he said. "Let's sneak over and see if we can find out what they're doing."

"No way," M.E. said. "If he catches us, he'll probably want to throw us off the tram like he did Matt the Brat."

"But I think Quinn's right," Luke said. "He seems nervous, and he keeps looking around. I definitely think he's up to something"

"Maybe," Mika said, "but I think we should stay away from him."

"Well, I'm going over there," Luke said. He turned to the others. "Anyone coming with me?"

"I'll come," Cody said. "But we have to be careful. If he catches us, he'll make sure we get in trouble."

"And I don't want to miss the immigration station," Mika added.

Quinn nodded. "You two stay here," he told Mika and M.E. "We'll go find out what's up."

Luke gestured for Quinn and Cody to follow him. Hunkering down, they ducked behind a row of shrubs and crept along until they reached some trees. They inched closer until they were within hearing distance. Then Luke held up his hand—a military signal meaning "stop." He put his finger against his lips and peered out from behind the tree.

"This is all you're giving me?" Schnikey said to the other man, whose back was to the kids. "After the risks I took to get you all this stuff? If I get caught in that restricted area, I could get fired, you know."

"Yeah, well, I need you to keep it up," the man said. "I'm not making enough money on the stuff you give me. And you're not the only one taking a risk."

Cody leaned forward to hear better and accidentally rustled the bushes.

The two men turned toward the sound where the kids were hiding.

The Code Busters remained frozen to the spot.

"What was that?" said the other man.

Schnikey shrugged. "Just critters. Most likely raccoons or deer. Don't worry, that school group is doing some kind of scavenger hunt. I wouldn't have signaled you to meet here if I didn't think it was safe."

Cody remembered the blinking light she'd seen from the ferry as it neared Angel Island. So that *was* a signal! Morse code! What were these guys up to? Whatever it was, it sure didn't sound good.

Cody peeked out from the tree again. The mystery man turned around—and Cody almost gasped when she saw the tattoo on the man's arm. She'd seen it before!

"Look, I have to get back now," said Schnikey. "Those brats expect me to finish driving them around the island."

Luke signaled frantically to the others.

Code Busters Key and Solution found on pp. 168 and 177.

Following Luke's lead, Cody and Quinn crept back along bushes until they were out of sight of Mr. Schnikey. They met up with M.E. and Mika, who looked relieved to see them.

"What happened?" M.E. asked. "We couldn't see you guys after you disappeared behind those trees. We thought maybe you got caught!"

Mika added, "Did you find out anything?"

"There's definitely something going on between Schnikey and some other guy," Luke said as they headed for the tram. "Schnikey gave this other dude something, and then the guy gave him a wad of money. And they were acting really suspicious."

"You're lucky they didn't see you," Mika said. "If they had, you could have been in real trouble." She turned to Quinn and smiled shyly. "I'm glad you didn't get caught."

"Me too," Quinn said, standing up a little straighter.

Cody glanced at M.E., trying not to smile. Did Mika have a crush on Quinn? Cody didn't know whether to be more surprised at that or at what she'd discovered about the man Schnikey had been talking to.

By the time the Code Busters got back on the tram, Delbert Schnikey was in his seat, frowning, as usual. As the kids sat down, he scanned the passengers in his mirror. Suddenly he focused on Cody. Cody quickly looked away. Maybe it was just her imagination. Or did Schnikey know the Code Busters had been spying on him?

The tram pulled away and continued its journey to their final destination. Cody turned in her seat and signed to the others so Schnikey wouldn't know what she was saying:

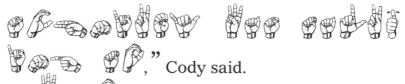

," Cody said.

"?" Luke and Quinn signed at the same time, circling their mouths with their index fingers.

"."

Quinn pointed to Cody, then moved his index finger out from his chin, the signs for "You sure?"

Cody nodded. "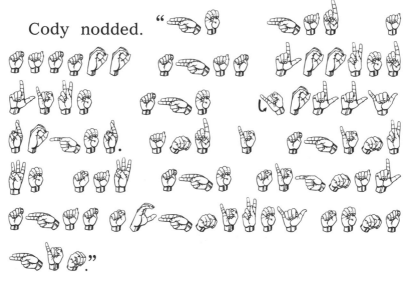"

Code Busters Key and Solution found on pp. 171 and 178.

The Code Busters exchanged glances.

"Well," Luke said aloud, "this is getting weirder and weirder."

Chapter 7

It was a short ride to the immigration station, an old building that had once housed hundreds of families who wanted to live in America. Cody was eager to see inside the place and find the poems left by former residents.

As soon as the tram came to a stop, Delbert Schnikey hopped off, while Ranger Yee stood up and began the last part of her talk.

"The immigration station was built in 1905 here in China Cove. Believe it or not, immigrants came from eighty-four different countries, but most were Chinese, and many others were Japanese. The building was actually more of a detention center, since many Chinese people were not welcome in the country. When the first immigrants arrived here around 1848, about the time gold was discovered in California, they were not allowed to look for gold. Instead, they were forced to do difficult, dangerous jobs like building the Central Pacific Railroad. Then in 1882, a new law made it very hard for Chinese people to come here at all."

Wow, thought Cody. It was hard to believe that some people weren't let into the country just because they were Chinese. If that were still true, Quinn and several of her other friends might not be here.

"After the law was passed," the ranger continued, "you could only enter the country if your father was already a US citizen. Even then, many of those people had to go through difficult interrogations that could last for hours, days, even weeks. While they waited, they often carved poems into the wooden walls to kill time and express their feelings. You'll see some of these poems as we tour the building."

"I think my great-great-grandfather left some

poems," Mika whispered to Cody and M.E. "I hope I can find them."

Ranger Yee pointed down the hill to the two-story building. "That's where the immigrants were kept."

Cody spotted the building, a short steep walk down a wide cement path.

"After World War II," Ranger Yee said, "the station was supposed to be demolished, but instead, the building was restored and turned into a museum. When you go inside, you'll get to see how the immigrants actually lived. They were crammed together in beds only a foot apart, stacked three high, with no privacy at all."

Cody couldn't imagine living that way. She was lucky to have her own bedroom where she could keep all her stuff, read, listen to music, and be alone if she wanted some space.

"Now, if you'll follow me, we'll head down the hill to the immigration station," Ranger Yee announced.

The students disembarked the tram—all but Matt and his chaperone-buddy—and took the steep path to the building that overlooked some steps, a courtyard, and a sweeping view of the bay. Once everyone was assembled at the front of the building, Ms. Stad and Mr. Pike handed each student another sheet of paper.

"All right, students, this is your final set of coded clues," Ms. Stad said. "Once you've solved the message, take a picture of the item. Then hand in your materials to us when we return to camp. Remember to stay with your buddy while on the tour, and don't leave the building."

The Code Busters looked at their papers. If this was a code message, it was completely new to Cody.

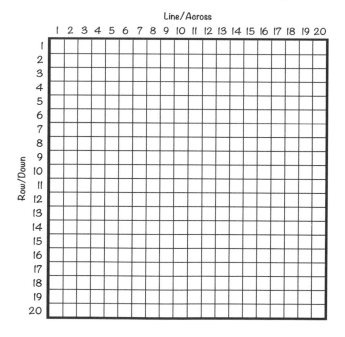

2-3 2-4 2-7 2-10 2-12 2-13 2-14

3-2 3-5 3-7 3-10 3-13

4-2 4-7 4-8 4-9 4-10 4-13 4-16 4-17 4-18

5-2 5-5 5-7 5-10 5-13

6-3 6-4 6-7 6-10 6-12 6-13 6-14

8-2 8-5 8-7 8-8 8-9 8-12 8-13 8-14 8-16
  8-17 8-18

9-2 9-3 9-5 9-7 9-11 9-16

10-2 10-4 10-5 10-7 10-8 10-9 10-12 10-13
  10-16 10-17 10-18

11-2 11-5 11-7 11-14 11-16

12-2 12-5 12-7 12-8 12-9 12-11 12-12 12-13
  12-16 12-17 12-18

14-2 14-3 14-4 14-8 14-9 14-12 14-13 14-14
  14-16 14-20

15-2 15-5 15-7 15-10 15-12 15-16 15-17
  15-19 15-20

16-2 16-3 16-4 16-7 16-10 16-12 16-13 16-14
  16-16 16-18 16-20

17-2 17-7 17-10 17-12 17-16 17-20

18-2 18-8 18-9 18-12 18-13 18-14 18-16 18-20

Code Busters Solution found on pp. 172 and 178.

Cody read the name of the puzzle written at the top of the worksheet. "It's called a nonogram."

"Never heard of it," Luke said.

"I have!" Mika spoke up. "These are popular puzzles in Japan. Usually the numbers on the top and side tell you how many squares to fill in, but not where, so they're kind of hard. But this one seems easier. It looks like you just blacken the squares that match the numbers. See the first number on the list—two dash three?"

The kids nodded.

"That means row 2, line 3," Mika said. "Blacken the square that matches those coordinates."

Cody did as directed.

"Just keep going, matching the numbers to the squares, and see what appears. Usually it's a picture of something, probably the thing we're supposed to take a snapshot of."

The Code Busters worked on their puzzles, filling in the grid according to the numbers. For a few minutes, Cody didn't recognize anything, but after blackening a few more squares, she realized what the puzzle meant.

"Cool!" Cody said, holding up the finished solution. The others compared their puzzles to hers. All of them had gotten the same answer. "I guess we're supposed to take a picture of one of these. Now we have to find one."

"And maybe we'll find my great-grandfather's puzzle box while we look!" said Mika.

As the students entered the building, Mika could barely contain her excitement. The group passed the rangers' office, where an elderly man in a brown suit sat behind a desk, working on some papers. In a corner of the room, drinking a soda, was Delbert Schnikey.

That was fast, Cody thought. *He must know every shortcut on the island since he beat us here.*

The old man at the desk smiled, rose slowly, and followed the group into a large empty room beyond the office.

"Students," Ranger Yee began as soon as everyone quieted down. "I'd like you to meet Mr. Edward Chan. He'll be your guide through the museum."

Cody noticed Mr. Chan was very short—shorter than most of the kids. His straight, graying hair was neatly combed, and he wore frameless glasses.

"Mr. Chan arrived on the island with his parents when he was a small child," the ranger continued, "so he's very familiar with what life was like here. Please welcome him."

The students clapped, and Mr. Chan bowed.

Folding his hands in front of him, he began. "Thank you for visiting the immigration station on Angel Island." His voice was soft, and he pronounced his words carefully. "Please follow me to the next room, where you'll find the living quarters. That is where hundreds of men, women, and children were housed—although the men were kept separate from the women and children. Once we're all there, I'll tell you stories about what it was like living here in those days."

The students quietly entered the men's dormitory. Cody was surprised to see the room filled nearly to the ceiling with cots that looked like triple bunk beds. Mr. Chan explained that each man was given a cot, a pillow, and a blanket. Cody spotted some other random items on the cots too—a pair of worn shoes, eyeglasses, a few faded snapshots of family members, and articles of clothing. She raised her hand and asked about them.

"Those are items the immigrants left behind when they finally left the island," Mr. Chan answered. "We kept them and put them on display so you could see some of the things they brought with them to America."

Cody wondered how the immigrants could have forgotten these important items. Maybe they never had a chance to collect their things before they left the island. After all, Mika's great-great-grandparents hadn't had time to retrieve the last hidden puzzle box.

Mr. Chan continued to share stories of life on the island. Once he was finished, he told the kids to look around if they wished but to stay behind the rope barrier, touch nothing, and not leave the room.

Mika pointed at some carved characters on one of the walls. Cody squinted at them. The symbols looked as if they had been covered with several layers of thick paint.

"I see you have found some of the poems left behind by the immigrants," Mr. Chan said, noticing Mika and Cody staring at the poem.

"As you can see," Mr. Chan explained, "the poems were once covered over in paint, but they were discovered after renovations began. We quickly learned that people had written poems about their experiences and feelings while they were confined on the island, separated from their loved ones." He turned to the poem Mika had been looking at and translated it:

This is a message to those who live here not to worry too much.
Instead, you must cast your useless worries to the flowing stream.
Experiencing a little trouble is not hardship.

Cody felt sorry for the person who'd written the poem. Even though it sounded hopeful, there was a feeling of sadness. She wished she could read the Chinese characters so she could understand all the poems written on the walls. They were beautifully carved and perfectly square, and they looked more like artwork than poetry.

"This has to be the last item on the scavenger hunt," Cody told the others. They got out their smartphones and took pictures.

Mika raised her hand. "Have you ever heard of a poet named Senjin?" she asked Mr. Chan.

He shook his head. "I'm sorry. I have not. Did you have a relative on the island at one time?"

Mika nodded. "My great-great-grandfather. He was Japanese, and he was on Angel Island for a while. I just wondered if he might have written a poem on one of these walls too."

"Most of these poems are Chinese," Mr. Chan said. "But you never know. I'm sure other immigrants wrote poems or messages that were eventually covered up as well. I've seen some Japanese characters on the baseboards, but I can't make them out."

Mika began to walk around the room, looking

down at the baseboards that lined the walls close to the floor. Cody figured she was searching for some kind of clue that her great-great-grandfather might have left for his wife while they were here.

"Find anything?" Cody asked Mika after she'd finished touring the room.

"No," Mika said, looking disappointed, "but since this dormitory was just for men, I don't think Hiraku would have left a message for his wife here." She looked off to the side where a staircase led to the second floor. A rope strung across it read NO ADMITTANCE.

"I wonder what's upstairs," Mika said.

"None of your business," came a gravelly voice behind the Code Busters. Delbert Schnikey stood with his hands on his hips, looking as crabby as usual. "You're not allowed anywhere but this floor, so stay with your group or you'll have to leave. That goes for the basement as well."

"She wasn't *going* up there," Quinn spoke up. "She was just *wondering*, that's all."

Mika gave Quinn a shy smile.

Schnikey made a guttural noise that sounded like a dragon clearing its throat. Before he could say anything else, Mr. Chan called the students to attention. "Please follow me to the community room."

Delbert Schnikey eyed the kids as they headed for the next room. When the unpleasant tram driver was out of sight, Cody turned to Mika. "Maybe we'll find something in here." Cody glanced around at the large, windowless room, sparsely furnished with only a couple of rickety wooden tables and chairs. A tattered deck of cards sat on one of the tables, along with some old newspapers written in what Cody guessed was Mandarin. Along the wall was a row of well-worn, graffiti-covered benches. With so little in the room, Cody wondered what the immigrants did in here, other than play cards and read the newspaper.

"As you can see," Mr. Chan began, "the community room didn't have much to offer, but it gave the immigrants a chance to escape their cramped dormitories and perhaps play a game of mah-jongg, read, or talk about the old country."

Cody spotted Mika roaming the room again. She appeared to be checking out the walls, baseboards, and even the floor. Finally, she sat down on one of the worn wooden benches, looking glum. The other Code Busters joined her.

"No luck?" Cody asked.

Mika shook her head.

"Hmmm," Quinn said. "If I wanted to send a message to someone but didn't want anyone else to see it, where would I leave it?"

The kids thought for a moment and then Luke said, "How about under something, like one of the benches?"

The kids checked under each of the benches but found nothing.

"Or one of the tables?" M.E. suggested.

Mika headed for the large table where a deck of cards lay. She bent over and looked underneath the table, then covered her mouth and straightened up.

"Did you find something?" Cody asked, feeling the hairs on her neck tingle as she joined her.

"It's a haiku in Japanese!" Mika whispered

breathlessly. "And it's signed *Senjin*! I think I've found a message from my great-great-grandfather!"

"What does it say?" M.E. asked.

Mika translated the Japanese characters into English.

Seek the place that nourishes
Body but not soul.
Find, behind the flame, my gift.

"What the heck is that supposed to mean?" Luke said.

"I bet the gift is a puzzle box he left for my great-great-grandmother," said Mika. "And the rest of the poem is a clue about where to find it. But what does the clue mean?"

Before anyone could come up with an answer, Ms. Stad called out. "All right, students, it's time to head back to camp."

Mika's face fell. "But we haven't had time to figure out the message!"

"Let's take a picture of it!" said Cody. "Then we'll

work on it when we get back to camp." Cody tried to reassure her friend as the students began to file out of the room.

"But we're not coming back here!" Mika cried. "How am I going to find the box he mentioned in the poem?"

"Hey!" came a booming voice behind them. "What were you kids doing with that table?" It was Delbert Schnikey, standing right behind them, his hands on his hips. He looked even crabbier than he had earlier. "And what's all this talk about some hidden box?"

The Code Busters looked at one another.

Then Quinn said, "Lima-echo-tango-sierra golf-echo-tango Oscar-uniform-tango Oscar-foxtrot Hotel-echo-romeo-echo!"

Code Busters Key and Solution found on pp. 171 and 178.

Chapter 8

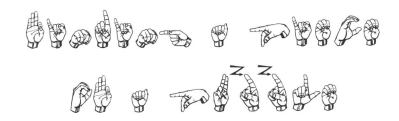

Cody knew Mika was reluctant to leave the immigration station without finding more from her great-great-grandfather, but on the tram ride back to camp, Cody promised her friend that the Code Busters would work on the puzzle. Maybe they could find an answer if they studied it together.

After the students arrived at the campsite, they handed over their scavenger hunt answer sheets, along with details of each photograph they'd taken. After a campfire dinner of hot dogs, corn on the cob, salad, and s'mores, the students listened to Ranger Yee's stories of the Miwok Indians. She even taught them some American Indian sign language, which Cody loved.

With an hour before bedtime, the students were free to read, listen to music, or play games in their tents. Cody, M.E., and Mika headed for Quinn and Luke's tent to work on Mika's haiku puzzle.

Quinn got out his Code Busters notebook and a pencil. "Okay, let's figure this out." He reread the poem aloud.

Seek the place that nourishes
Body but not soul.
Find, behind the flame, my gift.

"It definitely seems to be talking about something Senjin hid," said M.E.

"So what's a place that nourishes the body?" Luke asked.

"Someplace with food," guessed Mika.

"And a place that also has a flame?" Quinn added.

"What kind of flame?" Mika said. "A campfire? A fireplace?"

"It could be a stove," M.E. said. "You'd find a stove in a place that has food."

"I think you're right!" Quinn said. "A place with a stove and food has to be . . ."

". . . a kitchen!" Mika squealed, finishing the sentence for him.

Cody hushed her and peered out of the tent, checking to see if Matt the Brat or anyone else had heard them talking. The coast looked clear, but she couldn't be absolutely sure. She decided to use sign language with the others, just in case.

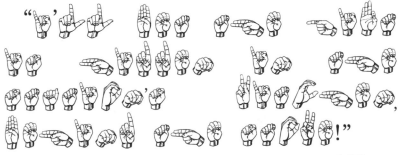

Code Busters Key and Solution found on pp. 171 and 179.

"We have to go there!" Mika said, again too loud. Cody hushed her again.

Mika whispered, "But it makes sense. That's one place both men and women would go, even if it was at different times. My great-great-grandfather could have left something there for her to find."

"But do you really think it might still be there, after all these years?" M.E. asked.

"I don't know," Mika said, shrugging, "but I have to find out."

Quinn smiled at her, looking impressed by her determination. "Okay, we need a plan."

Just as the Code Busters finished devising their plan to find the hidden object, Ms. Stad called, "Lights out! Everyone back to your own tent!"

The girls packed up their notebooks; said good night to the boys; and headed for their tent, using their phone flashlights to find their way in the dark. They went to the latrine, put on their pajamas, and slithered into their sleeping bags. Ms. Stad and Mr. Pike announced they'd be around to check on everyone. Now all the Code Busters had to do was wait.

"Are you sure you really want to do this?" M.E. whispered after Ms. Stad had stopped by to see if the girls were snuggled in their bags.

Cody knew M.E. was scared and probably having second thoughts about their plan, but she also knew how important it was to Mika to find her ancestor's hidden gift, whatever it was.

"Don't worry, M.E.," Cody reassured her. "It will only take us about ten minutes to get there. We'll sneak inside, run upstairs, check behind the stove, and get back here in less than a half hour."

"But what if there are a bunch of wild animals that come out at night?" M.E. said.

"The only animals on Angel Island are deer, raccoons, and birds, remember?"

"And snakes," M.E. mumbled. "And rats. And spiders."

Mika shook her head. "M.E., you don't have to go. Seriously. This is my idea, and I don't want anyone to get in trouble."

"I know," M.E. sighed. "I'm coming. I just hope nothing bad happens."

Cody nodded. She knew M.E. was a worrier, but Cody was sure they'd be there and back in no time.

A light flashed in through the tent screen. Cody got out her notebook and copied down the Morse code message as the light blinked on and off from the boys' tent.

•—• • •— —•• —•——?

•—• • •— —•• —•——! Cody answered, using the flashlight app on her phone.

—— • • —
—••• • •••• •• —• —••
— •••• •
•—•• •— — •—• •• —• •
•• —• ••—• •• •••— •
—— •• —• ••— — • •••

the boys' message said.

— • —• - ••—• ——— ••— •—•

replied Cody, using the police code for "message received."

—••• •
—•—• •— •—• • ••—• ••— •—••
the boys warned.

—●— — —— — ●●— — ——— ———

replied Cody.

Code Busters Key and Solution found on pp. 167 and 179.

"It's time!" Cody whispered to M.E. and Mika. The girls put their clothes on over their pajamas and puffed up their sleeping bags with extra clothes in case the teachers came to check on them again. Cody glanced outside to make sure no one was around. She didn't see anyone and only heard the hooting of an owl and the rustle of the leaves in the trees. At least, she hoped they were just leaves. Leading the way, she tiptoed carefully toward the latrine, with Mika and M.E. right behind her.

Quinn and Luke were already there, waiting for them.

"Did anyone see you?" Quinn whispered to the girls.

"No," Cody whispered back. "But let's do this fast. We'll be in real trouble if we get caught. It won't be easy to explain why we left our tents."

They were about to start up the path toward the

immigration station when Cody heard the crack of a twig. *That was no raccoon,* she thought. Something much bigger was moving around in the nearby trees.

M.E. grabbed Cody's arm. "What was that?" she whispered.

The sound came again. M.E. squeezed Cody's arm tighter.

The kids froze, listening. After a minute passed quietly—except for the sound of Cody's thumping heartbeat—she let out her breath. Luke whispered, "Probably just a deer. Nothing to worry about. Let's go."

The five Code Busters began climbing the steep hill that led to the immigration station, using their cell phones to light the way. They were winded by the time they reached the entrance and took a moment to catch their breaths.

Cody checked her watch. Ten minutes had passed. They were right on time. If everything went according to plan, they'd be back in their sleeping bags in another twenty minutes.

Quinn pointed to a light in the front window of

the building. "That must be the office." He crept up and peered in, then turned to the group.

"Schnikey's in there, but it looks like he's sound asleep in his chair," he whispered to the others.

"I wonder what he's doing there," Cody said.

"I bet he's supposed to be guarding the building, but he's not doing a very good job. Let's go around back and see if we can get in that way."

The kids followed Quinn as he lit his way along the side of the building. When they reached the back door, Quinn tried the knob. It didn't budge.

"Locked," he said. "How are we going to get in? This place is like a prison."

Mika said, "I think we'll have to go in through the front. Maybe it won't be locked, since Schnikey is there. But we'll have to be really quiet if we're going to get past him."

Cody wasn't so sure about this part of the plan, but she agreed when the others nodded. This looked like their only option.

They returned to the front entrance, and Quinn slowly turned the knob.

The door opened.

They listened for a few seconds and then heard the unusually loud sound of snoring coming from the office, just down the hallway. To Cody, it sounded like a machine gun going off inside a tunnel. She wondered how Schnikey could sleep through all that noise he was making.

Quinn opened the door wider but stopped when he heard it creak. Then, timing it to Schnikey's snores, he inched it open a little at a time, until the kids could fit through.

One by one, they tiptoed past the open office door, making sure to step on the old wooden boards only when Schnikey snored. Once they'd made it to the other end of the hallway without waking him, they located the staircase. It was blocked off with rope and a sign that read NO ADMITTANCE. Another faded sign painted on the wall read MESS HALL. An arrow pointed up.

"That must be where the kitchen is," M.E. whispered to the others.

They headed up the stairs, stepping over the rope

and taking each step slowly and carefully. Cody, bringing up the rear, paused to listen once more for Schnikey's snores. Certain he was still asleep, she joined the others.

When they reached the top of the stairs, Cody looked around. She was disappointed to find the room was basically empty. It was hard to tell what it had been like in Senjin's time. She spotted more poems carved into the walls, but otherwise, the place was bare.

Cody saw disappointment on Mika's face as well. "We might as well look around," Cody said, and Mika nodded. They started walking slowly around the room, shining their phone along the walls. Luke, who had been staring at the wall, pointed to a large rectangular area that looked lighter than the wall around it. "See that spot? I'll bet the stove used to be there."

Mika bent down and examined the space. She shined her phone light over the floorboards near it.

"Oh my gosh!" she whispered. "Look at this!"

The others bent down to examine the board Mika

was touching with her fingertips. In the light from their phones, Cody could see some scratches on it.

"What?" M.E. asked. "They're just scratches."

"No, they're Japanese characters. This says *Senjin*!"

Cody noticed the board looked a little warped, while the other boards were pretty flat.

"Luke," she whispered, "is there any way you can pull up that board? It looks like it might be loose."

Luke reached into his pocket and pulled out his keys. Using one of the keys, he began digging at the edge of the board. Seconds later, he yanked the warped board from the floor, revealing a four- or five-inch hole underneath.

Mika gasped.

Inside, undisturbed for decades and covered in cobwebs, was a small box, about the size of half a cube of butter. It was made of tiny pieces of wood that had been put together in an intricate design and carved with Japanese characters.

"I think we've found my great-great-grandfather's Koyosegi puzzle box!" Mika picked it up and brushed away the cobwebs. But before she could open it, Cody held up her hand, her eyes wide.

The kids froze. Then Quinn asked "?" in sign language.

Cody pointed to her ear, then fingerspelled.

Code Busters Key and Solution found on pp. 171 and 179.

Before they could move, the open door to the mess hall slammed shut with a loud bang.

Luke ran to the door and tried the knob. It wouldn't move. The door was locked.

The Code Busters were trapped inside!

Chapter 9

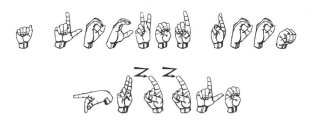

Luke tried the door again, ramming his shoulder into it. It still didn't budge. "Shh!" said Quinn. "You'll wake Schnikey!"

"Ahoy, mates!" came a familiar voice from the other side of the door. "It's Davy Jones' locker for ye swabs!"

The Code Busters looked at one another.

"Matt?" they all said at the same time.

"Ho ho ho and a bottle of bilgewater!" came the reply in a bad pirate accent.

"Matthew Jeffreys!" Cody said, "You let us out of here right now, or I'm telling Ms. Stad!"

"Oh yeah?" Matt said. "What're ya gonna tell her? That you sneaked out of camp and came here in the middle of the night? No problem. She'll find out soon enough, when I get back and tell her you've all run away! Man, you guys are going to be in trouble then!"

Cody shook her head. Luke tried the door again.

"It's no use," M.E. moaned. "He must have locked it from the other side. What are we going to do?"

"*MATT!*" Quinn yelled. "Unlock this door— now!—and let us out!"

Cody winced. Apparently Quinn wasn't worried about waking Delbert Schnikey anymore.

"Sorry, sea-rats, but my ship is sailing soon," Matt the Pirate replied. "Gotta shove off. Been nice knowin' ya!"

The kids heard Matt's heavy footsteps as he lumbered down the stairs. Surely Schnikey would wake up now.

Suddenly the kids heard a loud crash, followed by a shriek.

"What was that?" M.E. asked, looking terrified.

No one answered.

Cody waited, listening, but there was no other sound. Only dead silence.

Luke shrugged. "Matt's just trying to scare us."

"Maybe Mr. Schnikey heard him and will come rescue us," Mika said.

"Maybe," Luke said, "but I think we'd better try to figure out a way to escape on our own. Schnikey isn't the nicest guy on the planet."

Cody had to admit she didn't like the thought of the crabby caretaker finding them up here.

The Code Busters searched the room for another exit, but the only other door was nailed shut.

"There has to be a fire escape," Cody said. "All buildings have fire codes."

"Not really old ones," Quinn said. "This place was probably built before they thought of anything like that."

"What about the window?" Mika said, pointing to a dirty-paned glass window next to an ancient, rusted radiator. The kids ran over to it, and Luke tried to push it open. "Oh great! It's stuck!"

"Is there a lock that we're not seeing?" asked M.E.

"Nope." Cody pointed to the edges of the window. "It's just been painted so often that the paint has sealed it shut."

"Luke, what about your keys?" Mika said. "Maybe one of them could loosen the windowsill."

Luke pulled his keys out of his jeans pocket again. "Good thing my grand-mere makes me keep these. They sure come in handy."

"Yeah, except for unlocking that door," Quinn added.

Luke dug at the crevices along the window's edges, slowly carving away the thick paint. Then he tried lifting the window again. "Ta-da!" he announced as the window inched up a crack. A few more tugs and grunts, and the window opened wide enough for the kids to fit through.

They leaned over and looked out.

It was at least a twelve-foot drop from the second story onto the pavement below.

"No way," Quinn said. "We can't jump. The fall

will probably kill us."

Cody had an idea. "Take off your jackets," she told the others, as she peeled off her own red hoodie.

"Why?" M.E. said. "It's freezing in here."

Cody reached for M.E.'s jacket. "We'll tie the arms together and use the jackets like a rope to climb down. I saw it in a movie once where these prisoners tied their bedsheets together and escaped. We can tie off the last one here." She pointed to the radiator, which probably hadn't been used to heat the room in years. She just hoped it would stay anchored to the floor and hold their weight as they shimmied down the side of the building.

"It's worth a try," Luke said, tying the sleeve of his athletic jacket to the sleeve of M.E.'s jacket. Quinn and Mika handed their jackets to Luke, and he finished tying all five together, making sure the knots were secure.

"Okay," he said, "I think they're strong enough."

"You *think*?" M.E. said, crossing her arms over her chest to keep out the cold. She was starting to shiver.

Luke tied the end of Cody's hoodie sleeve to the radiator and tugged to see if the old heater would stand firm. "So far, so good. So who's going first?"

"M.E.?" Quinn suggested. "You're the littlest."

"Thanks a lot," M.E. said, frowning. "So if I fall, you'll know the plan's not working, right?"

Quinn grinned at her. "Right! So try not to fall."

M.E. stuck out her tongue at Quinn.

Luke looked out the window again, then pulled his head back in. "Listen, there's a drainpipe right next to the window," he said to M.E. "Hold on to it as we let you down."

"And when you get to the ground, give us a thumbs-up to let us know you're OK," added Cody. "Don't call out, or Schnikey might hear you."

M.E. nodded as Luke began tying the other end of the jacket-rope around M.E's small waist. When it was secure, she hoisted one leg over the sill and ducked under the window. Gripping the drainpipe to steady herself, she pulled her other leg over, while Luke and Quinn held the other end of the jackets. Slowly they let the line out, lowering M.E.

inch by inch. Cody watched as M.E. half dangled along the side of the building, her face frozen with fear.

Moments later, to Cody's relief, M.E. was safely on the ground. She looked up at the others with a big smile and gave them a thumbs-up.

Luke pulled the jacket-rope up and repeated the process with Mika, Cody, and then Quinn, carefully lowering them down to the pavement. After Quinn untied himself and gave the thumbs-up, Luke looked out the window at the others and frowned.

"Uh-oh," Cody whispered. "How's he going to get down? There's no one to hold the jackets for him on the other end."

"Duh!" Quinn said, slapping his forehead. "Why didn't I think of this before?" He dug his cell phone out of his pocket. "I need your phone," he said to Cody.

"You're going to call him?" Cody asked in confusion, handing over her phone. "With two phones?"

"Nope," he whispered. Clicking on the flashlight apps on his and Cody's cell phones, he held them at arm's length and then moved his arms into different positions.

Cody realized Quinn was sending a semaphore to Luke on the second floor. Brilliant! That way, he wouldn't wake Schnikey by yelling up at Luke. Still, Cody nervously wondered how the guard could have slept through everything that had happened already.

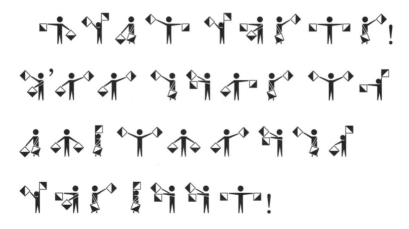

Code Busters Key and Solution found on pp. 168 and 179.

Luke flashed a thumbs-up, tossed down the jackets, and stepped away from the window. Quinn took off running toward the front of the building. The others untied their jackets and pulled them on, zipping them up against the cold wind. Moments later, the two boys were back.

"Let's get out of here," Quinn whispered.

The kids turned to go—and froze.

A wide-awake Delbert Schnikey stood in front of them, a crooked snarl creasing his mouth.

"Sooooo. The little snoops are back!" Schnikey said, raising the flashlight he held in one hand and shining the beam at their faces. Cody was nearly blinded by the light and tried to shade her eyes.

"Mr. Schnikey," Cody tried to explain, "I know this must look bad, but we were just trying to find something that belongs to Mika and—"

"Shut up!" Schnikey boomed. "This is *my* island, and everything on it belongs to me. I'm not about to have you brats ruining my business."

Cody frowned. "I don't know what you're talking about, Mr. Schnikey. Like I said, we were just trying to—"

"*Enough!*" Schnikey yelled at them. He pointed to the golf cart parked nearby. "Get in the cart, all of you! I'm taking you back to your camp and telling your teachers you're a bunch of vandals destroying state property. You'll end up in juvie by the time I'm done with you."

Cody knew all about juvie from her mother, who was a police officer. That was the last place she'd ever want to go.

"Come on!" Schnikey yelled even louder.

Cody didn't move. Instead, she held her finger up to her lips. "Did you hear that?" she said, staring back at the immigration station.

Nobody moved.

The sound came again.

●●● ━ ━ ━ ●●●

Code Busters Key and Solution found on pp. 167 and 179.

Tap-tap-tap. Then three more taps, this time slower. Then three quick taps again.

The kids instantly recognized the Morse code distress signal and looked at one another.

The faint signal came again.

Then again. And again.

"Someone's in trouble!" Cody said.

"I think it's coming from inside the building," Luke added.

Before Schnikey could stop them, the five kids ran back inside the immigration station.

Chapter 10

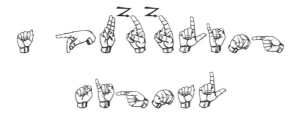

"It sounded like it came from over there," Quinn said, pointing at the staircase that had led them to the second floor.

The Code Busters ran toward the tinny, metallic sound that kept repeating the same sequence of taps—three short, three long, and three short. As they listened, Cody noticed that the sound seemed louder beneath her feet but still muffled. She knelt down and put her ear to the floor.

"The taps are coming from under here!" she said, getting back up.

The kids searched the area for an entrance that would lead downstairs, but no doors or other staircases were nearby. Then M.E. pointed to something on the floor behind the stairs.

"Guys! Check this out!" she cried.

Cody looked at the wood flooring and noticed a section about three feet square that didn't match the rest of the floorboards. She stamped on the square and then stamped on the wood flooring next to it. They sounded different.

"This part sounds hollow," she told the others.

Quinn pointed to a notch cut into one side of the square panel. He slid his hand inside—it fit perfectly.

"It's got to be a trapdoor!" he exclaimed. "This must be how you open it." He yanked on it, but it didn't budge. He stood up.

Luke knelt down and inserted his hand into the notch. He pulled and grunted too, trying to lift the trapdoor open, but it wouldn't give.

Thinking maybe Schnikey could help them open it, Cody glanced down the hallway to see if he had followed them inside, but there was no sign of him.

"Mr. Schnikey!" Cody called. "We need your help!"

Delbert Schnikey appeared in the doorway at the end of the hall. "What now?" he bellowed. "I told you kids to get in the cart."

"We think someone's trapped down in the basement!" Quinn said. "We heard the SOS distress code, but we can't get this trapdoor open."

Schnikey frowned at the group. "You really think someone's actually under there?" he said, his eyes narrowing. "Well, that's impossible. No one's been down in that basement for decades. As long as I've been here, that trapdoor has never been opened."

"But we heard something and I think we should check it out," Luke said. He looked at the other Code Busters. "Remember that scream we heard just after Matt locked us in? Maybe he fell in there somehow—and he's trapped."

"I'm telling you, there's no one there," Schnikey said. "Now come on!"

Luke crossed his arms. "We're not leaving until we make sure." The others agreed.

Schnikey scratched his head, stroked his stubbly chin, and sighed. "All right. Move back. I'll see if I can open it and prove to you that no one's down there. Then we're going back to your camp."

The kids nodded.

Schnikey knelt down next to the trapdoor, spat on his hands, and rubbed them together. Cody grimaced and reminded herself not to touch anything that Schnikey had touched, in case he had a habit of spitting on lots of things.

Using both hands and bracing himself with one foot, he yanked at the door. It creaked open an inch or two, then slammed back down. Cody could tell the door was heavy, but at least it wasn't permanently shut. Schnikey gave the door another yank, and this time, it swung up and over, landing with a loud thud.

The Code Busters leaned over and peered into the pitch-black basement below.

"Hello?" Cody called into the opening.

They listened. No response.

"I don't see anything," M.E. said, squinting into the darkness.

Cody pulled out her phone and aimed the flashlight into the black hole.

Something moved.

"Rats!" M.E. squealed as she pulled back in horror. "The basement is full of rats!"

"It's probably just a few spiders," Cody said, trying to reassure her.

"I hate spiders!" M.E. replied.

Suddenly the tap-tap-tapping rang out again, this time louder as metal hit metal. Cody turned her phone light in the direction of the sound and gasped.

Eight feet below, a body lay on the ground. Barely moving.

"It's Matt!" she cried.

"It looks like he's hurt," Mika said.

"We've got to get him out of there," Luke said. He turned to Schnikey. "Is there another entrance to the basement besides this trapdoor?"

"Not that I know of," Schnikey said, shrugging.

"Do you have a ladder?"

"Nope. But I know how you can help him. Look

down there." Schnikey pointed into the darkness, lit only by Cody's phone light.

The kids leaned over to see what Schnikey meant.

A split second later, Cody felt herself being pushed through the opened trapdoor. She tumbled down to the floor, her fall broken by something soft.

She seemed to have landed on some sort of couch—and on top of Matt. Matt groaned loudly.

Suddenly M.E. screamed. A moment later, she landed on the couch right beside Cody.

Next came Mika.

Then Quinn.

Then Luke.

One by one, they'd been pushed into the hole in the floor. It all happened in a matter of seconds.

As the kids lay in a heap, moaning and groaning, Cody caught a glimpse of the only light coming from above. The last thing she saw was Delbert Schnikey's face as he held his flashlight with a gloved hand. And he was smiling.

The trapdoor slammed shut.

The room went blacker than black.

The Code Busters were trapped.

With a room full of spiders.

And an injured Matt the Brat.

*   *   *   *   *

Cody shook her head and blinked several times, hoping to clear her vision. But the darkness of the room was so dense that she couldn't see anything, not even her hand in front of her face. She heard grunting and shuffling as the others began to recover from the fall and shift their positions on the couch.

"Is everyone okay?" Mika's voice came from near Cody's right leg. Cody joined the chorus of groaned *yeahs* that answered Mika's question.

"What happened?" Cody asked.

"Schnikey! He pushed us!" Quinn said, to left of Cody.

"I tried to fight him, but he was too strong," said Luke.

"And I tried to run," said M.E. "But he caught me and threw me in."

Cody heard a long groan coming from directly

beneath her. She realized she was still sitting on top of Matt. She scrambled onto the floor, hoping she hadn't hurt him when she landed on him. "Matt? Are you all right?"

"Cody?" Matt wheezed. "Is that you?"

"Matt, what were you *doing* down here?" Cody asked him, wishing she could see his face.

"Somebody . . . pushed me," Matt moaned, "and I landed on my ankle. I think it's broken. It hurts real bad. I tried to signal for help . . ."

"We heard you," Cody said. "I didn't know you knew Morse code."

Matt grunted. "Just SOS."

Suddenly Luke's face lit up. He was holding his phone light on himself. "Listen, guys, we've got to think," he said, shining the light around at the others. "We have to get out of here before Schnikey comes back. Who knows what he's got planned for us?"

"Let's call for help," said Mika.

"My phone isn't getting any service," said Luke. "I was going to call for help, but this must be a dead zone."

Cody shivered at Luke's choice of words.

"I don't have any service either," M.E. added, tapping her cell phone.

Cody checked her pocket to see if she still had her phone, but it wasn't there. Then she remembered she'd been holding it and pointing the light into the basement when Schnikey told them to look down. She glanced around and spotted it lying a few feet away. Quickly, she snatched it, stood, and turned on the flashlight app. She shined the light around the room. Combined with the light from the others' phones, it revealed a sight she wasn't expecting. "Whoa. This basement sure doesn't look as if it's been abandoned for years, like Schnikey said."

A long worktable sat at one end of the room, filled with a bunch of rusty, worn tools. Cody recognized a hammer, drill, saw, and crowbar.

"Look at this!" Quinn said, picking up a weathered metal coin the size of a quarter. He moved his phone light to another cluttered area on the table. It was covered with old silver coins.

Luke picked up one of the coins and studied it

under his phone light. "It's dated 1549, and there's some kind of writing on it. I think it's Spanish. M.E., can you read this?"

M.E. took the coin, and Luke shined the light on it for her. "*Real de a ocho*," she said. "That means 'eight-piece coin.'"

"I knew it!" came a voice from the couch. Matt was now propped up on his elbow, his eyes wide with excitement. "Pieces of eight, from Drake's ship! We found the treasure!"

"Chill, Matt," Luke said. He held up a metal tray filled with small indentations the size of the coins. A similar one lay next to it on the worktable. "These coins are obviously counterfeit. Someone's been making them here in the basement, using those trays as molds. They're probably selling them to tourists and pretending they're real."

"Hey, there's other stuff here too," Mika said, holding up a couple of metal signs that read *Golden Hind*. "That's the name of Drake's ship," Quinn said. "Man, someone has quite a bogus business going down here. And I'm guessing it's

Schnikey. He knew this basement was here all along. He's probably working with the guy from the ferry. I'll bet Schnikey makes the fake stuff, and the other guy smuggles it off the island to sell to tourists."

"So that's what those two were doing when we saw them trading something in the woods," Mika said.

"Brrr," M.E. said, interrupting the excitement over the counterfeit discovery. "Did you guys feel that?"

"What?" Cody asked, shining her phone light at her friend.

"I just felt cold air on my face," M.E. said, glancing around. She frowned. "You don't think this place is . . . haunted, do you?"

"There's no such thing as ghosts," Cody reminded M.E. "But if you felt cold air, then there must be an opening somewhere. Where do you think it came from?"

M.E. paused, then turned and pointed to a darker part of the basement. "I just felt it again. It came from back there."

"Maybe it's a way out," Quinn said. "Schnikey has to have another access to this place besides the trapdoor. Let's see if we can find it!"

"Hey," Matt the Brat called out. "Don't leave me here alone!"

Four of the Code Busters headed in the direction M.E. indicated, while Cody stayed back with Matt. They both kept quiet. *Matt's foot must really hurt if he doesn't have the energy to say anything annoying*, Cody thought.

Moments later, Mika and Quinn returned. "Luke found a door!" Mika said. "They're trying to get it open, but they need something to smash the locked doorknob." She scanned the worktable and picked up the long, heavy crowbar. "This might work."

She ran back. Quinn remained with Cody and Matt. "We're going to have to help Matt get out of here," he said.

"Matt," Cody said to the boy who still lay propped up on the couch. "Can you get up?"

Matt pushed himself upright, wincing and moaning at every movement.

"Good," Cody said. "I'll take his right arm. Quinn, you take his left arm, and we'll lift him to standing.

Once we get him up, he can lean on us to walk so he doesn't have to use his sore foot."

Matt shook his head. "You guys can't help me. I'm way bigger than both of you together."

Cody made a face. "No, you're not. And yes, we can." She looked at Quinn. "Ready?"

He nodded.

"One, two, three—LIFT!" Cody commanded.

Using all their strength, Cody and Quinn hoisted Matt up, who grunted as he reached a standing position.

"Now wrap your arms around us and see if you can take a step," Cody ordered.

Matt did as he was told, keeping his right knee bent and his foot off the ground. Using the two Code Busters for support, he hopped forward on his other foot.

"Ow!" he said, his face creased in pain.

"You can do it!" Cody said encouragingly.

Slowly, they continued in the direction Mika had gone, Matt taking one hop at a time and groaning the whole way. When they reached the others, several yards ahead, they found Luke leaning on the crowbar he'd inserted into the side of a door. A metal doorknob lay on the floor in front of him. With one last push with the crowbar, the wooden door broke open.

"You did it!" M.E. squealed.

On the other side of the door was a set of stairs.

"Come on," Luke said. "We have to get out of here before Schnikey finds out we escaped. Cody, I'll take over for you."

Cody shook her head. "I'm fine. He's not that heavy."

Luke smiled at her. "All right, then follow me!"

Luke led everyone up the stairs. It wasn't easy getting Matt up to the top—or keeping him quiet so that they wouldn't attract Schnikey's attention—but Cody did her best to support his weight. Matt bit his lip and huffed and puffed, but to Cody's relief, he kept the groaning to a minimum.

Once they reached the top of the stairs, they spotted another door. Luckily, this one was unlocked. Quinn opened it, peered out, and then signed:

Code Busters Key and Solution found on pp. 171 and 179.

He headed for the ride, tiptoeing as he went, and then waved the others to follow him. Silently, Mika and M.E. hopped into the back, and then Quinn helped Matt squeeze in next to them. Luke and Cody shared the shotgun seat, while Quinn got into the driver's seat. He used the key that was still in the ignition to turn on the engine.

"HEY!" came a loud voice from behind them. Cody turned to see Delbert Schnikey running toward them. He was holding the crowbar they had used to free themselves from the basement.

"GO!" Luke ordered Quinn.

Quinn stepped on the pedal.

M.E. screamed as the cart took off with a jolt.

Cody held onto Luke, who held onto the side of the cart. She glanced back as Quinn steered the cart down the steep hill toward camp.

Schnikey stood scowling and shaking the crow-bar at them.

"I'll get you kids!" Cody heard him yell as he dis-appeared from sight.

Chapter 11

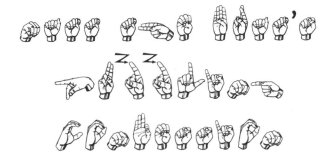

"Uh-oh," Cody said as the golf cart neared the campsite. Ms. Stad, Mr. Pike, and several chaperones were all holding lit flashlights and listening to Ranger Yee talk on her walkie-talkie. The ranger stopped when she spotted the kids heading straight for them.

"I-yay ink-thay e're-way in-yay ig-bay rouble-tay," Cody said in Pig Latin.

Code Busters Solution found on p. 180.

Quinn jerked the cart to a halt as soon as they reached the camp. The Code Busters climbed out, leaving Matt in the backseat.

Ms. Stad stepped forward. She didn't look happy. Not at all. "Where have you been?" Ms. Stad demanded, crossing her arms in front of her. "You knew you were not supposed to leave the camp! We were so worried! Ranger Yee was just about to contact the Coast Guard!"

Cody had never seen her teacher this angry— not even with Matt the Brat. She hoped that once she began explaining, Ms. Stad would calm down and understand.

"We're sorry, Ms. Stad, but we had a good reason. Honestly." Before she could say more, Matt the Brat spoke up.

"Yeah, sorry, Ms. Stad," Matt said quickly. "It's actually my fault. Don't blame them. They were just trying to help me." He glanced at the Code Busters.

They all stared at him, open-mouthed but unable to speak. Cody was in shock. This was a total surprise coming from Matt the Brat.

"What are you talking about, Matthew?" Ms. Stad asked, her frown deepening.

Cody had a sudden suspicious thought. What was Matt the Brat really up to? Did he plan to get the Code Busters in trouble by making up a story that was even worse than the truth?

"I was . . . I was sleepwalking," said Matt. "That's why I left my tent and the camp. I was actually sound asleep and didn't know what I was doing. But these guys saw me leave." He gestured toward the Code Busters. "And luckily, they followed me. Otherwise, I would've been stuck in the woods with a sprained ankle all night." He grinned at the Code Busters. "Thanks, guys."

Cody could hardly believe her ears. Why was Matt the Brat lying? Was he planning to blackmail them later? Or was he really trying to take the blame for the kids leaving camp? But why? Maybe he was trying to hide the fact that he'd been spying on them and following them, and that he'd locked them in the room on the second floor of the immigration station as a prank. Still, he really seemed to be covering for them. Cody was about to speak up and tell Ms. Stad the truth, but another golf cart suddenly pulled into the campground. It stopped just inches from where the Code Busters stood. The other students and chaperones who had gathered around to hear Matt's story gasped at how close the cart came to hitting them.

"What the . . ." Mr. Pike started to say.

Delbert Schnikey leaped out from behind the wheel, his face flushed with anger.

"You almost hit these kids!" Mr. Pike said, stepping toward him.

Schnikey ignored him. "*There* you are!" he hollered at the Code Busters. He turned to Ms. Stad. "Lady, I want these brats off the island first thing in the morning. Otherwise, I'll have them arrested for trespassing, destroying state property, attempted theft of valuable relics, and stealing a government vehicle! They should be locked up!"

Ranger Yee stepped forward. "Calm down, Delbert!" she ordered.

Ms. Stad's eyes went wide at Delbert Schnikey's

outburst. She glanced at Cody and the others. "Is this true?"

"No way!" Cody argued. "He's lying about everything! We didn't break into the building—the door was unlocked. We walked right in while he was sleeping on the job. We didn't damage anything—we just opened a window because we got locked inside and had to climb out to escape. And we didn't steal anything. He's the one who's a thief!" Cody pointed to Schnikey.

"What's this all about, Delbert?" demanded Ranger Yee.

"I told you!" he said. "They're a bunch of lying, thieving vandals, and I want them out of here!"

Ms. Stad turned to the tram driver. "Listen, Mr. Schnikey. My students don't lie, nor do they steal or vandalize property. When they tell me something, I believe them." She shot a look at Matt the Brat.

Ranger Yee eyed Schnikey. "Delbert, I want the truth now, or I'm calling the cops to come straighten this out."

"No need for that," Schnikey said, raising his

hands as if in surrender. He seemed to have a sudden change of heart after Ranger Yee's threat. "Just be sure these brats are gone first thing tomorrow, and I won't press charges."

"That's because you don't want anyone to find out what you've really been doing," Luke said.

"Yeah," Quinn added. "Then you'll have to explain why you have all those fake silver coins in the basement of the immigration station—like this one." Quinn pulled a coin from his pocket and handed it over to Ranger Yee. "Here's the proof. There's a bunch more back at Schnikey's secret workroom. He's been making the fake coins there."

"And he's been smuggling this fake Drake stuff off the island and selling it to tourists," Mika added.

Cody chimed in too. "He had help from a guy we saw on the ferry—someone with a pirate's flag tattoo."

Ranger Yee took the coin, studied it a moment, and then glared at Schnikey.

"Plus, he pushed us into the basement through a trapdoor and locked us in," M.E. said.

Ms. Stad, Mr. Pike, and Ranger Yee all stared at Delbert Schnikey.

"They're lying!" he said, taking a few steps back.

"We'll see about that," Ranger Yee said. She pulled her radio from her belt buckle and spoke into it: "This is Ranger Yee." The radio squawked, then a tinny voice replied, "Go ahead."

"I need backup at the campground, stat," she said.

"Ten-four" was the reply. Cody knew that meant "message received" in police code.

Ranger Yee replaced the radio in her belt. "It's about time I had a look in that basement. It was supposed to have been sealed off decades ago."

Schnikey backed up a few more paces, eyes wide with fear. Then he suddenly turned and bolted.

"He's getting away!" Mika shouted as Schnikey ran for the trees.

Ranger Yee shook her head. "Don't worry. He won't get far. I know this island like the back of my hand, and there's only one way off and on. We'll get him. I've called the other rangers and the Coast Guard, and I'll stay here at the camp until they arrive. Anyway, if what you say is true, I have a feeling he'll head for the basement and try to get rid of the counterfeit evidence. That'll be the first place we look. And we'll put a stop to any smuggling and sale of forgeries."

The Code Busters smiled until they saw Ms. Stad still glaring at them, one eyebrow raised. "You kids are not off the hook yet," she said, shaking her head. "You should have told one of the adults that Matt was sleepwalking and let us go after him."

The Code Busters exchanged glances. Cody thought about confessing the truth right then, but at that moment Matt groaned, reminding everyone he was in pain. Even though he had locked them in that room, she felt sorry for him. He'd ended up trapped in the dark basement with a bunch of spiders and who knew what else, plus he had hurt his foot.

"Matthew," Ms. Stad said, turning to the boy sitting in the chair and rubbing his foot. "I'm proud of you for taking responsibility, but we'll talk more after I do some research on somnambulism."

"Some what?" Matthew said, scrunching up his face at the long, unfamiliar word.

"Somnambulism," Ms. Stad repeated. "It means sleepwalking. I should think you'd know that since you claim to be a sleepwalker."

"Oh yeah," Matt said, squirming in his chair. "I forgot. Zombie-ism."

Cody stifled a laugh at Matt's mispronunciation of the word. After all, maybe sleepwalking was sort of like being a zombie.

"We'll discuss it in the morning over breakfast," Ms. Stad said. "Meanwhile, all of you, return to your tents and get some sleep."

As the Code Busters headed toward their tents, Mika whispered, "Should we tell Ms. Stad the whole truth about what happened?"

"Let's do it tomorrow," suggested Cody. "We'll find a way to do it without getting Matt into more trouble. After all, he did try to keep *us* out of trouble."

The boys returned to their tent and gave the girls a quick thumbs-up before closing the tent flap. The girls entered their own tent, closed the flap, and tied it securely.

A light began to flash on and off through the girls' mesh tent window.

"It's the boys," M.E. said, peering through the opening. "I think they're sending us a message in Morse code."

M.E. reached over and got her notebook and a pencil. She copied down the letters and read the message aloud.

Code Busters Key and Solution found on pp. 167 and 180.

Cody started to get out her cell phone and flash a message back in Morse code, until she heard Ms. Stad's booming voice: "I said LIGHTS OUT!"

"Uh-oh," M.E. whispered. "We'd better go to sleep. We can't afford to get into more trouble."

Mika sighed in the darkness. "I guess we'll

just have to wait until morning to find out what's inside the box." She tucked the small box under her pillow.

Cody closed her eyes, but after all that had happened, she knew it was going to take *forever* to fall asleep.

Chapter 12

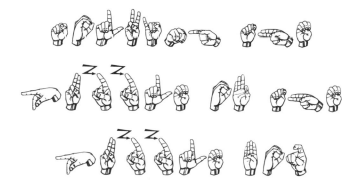

Morning came *way* too early for Cody. At first, she thought the whistle sound she heard was coming from her dream about being chased by evil tram drivers, but it turned out to be Ms. Stad's campground wake-up call.

Cody pushed herself up. She glanced at the other two sleeping bags and saw that her friends were still asleep.

"M.E.! Mika! Wake up!"

The other two girls groaned and stretched. Cody peered out the tent flap and checked the campground. The adults were standing around the campfire, drinking coffee, and talking. Among them was Ranger Yee, along with another ranger.

"I wonder if they've caught Schnikey yet," Cody said to the girls as they rubbed sleep from their eyes. "Come on! Let's find out what's happening."

They slithered out of their sleeping bags, put on their shoes, and climbed out of the tent. Mika held the small puzzle box in her hand.

"Did you catch Mr. Schnikey?" M.E. asked Ranger Yee as the girls joined the teachers, chaperones, and other rangers.

Ranger Yee nodded. "We found him hiding in the immigration station basement, just as we expected. He's in custody. The Coast Guard took him to the authorities early this morning."

The boys appeared, already changed out of their PJs. Mika gave Quinn a shy smile, and he grinned back.

"Did you find all the stuff he was making?" Luke asked the ranger.

"We sure did," Ranger Yee said. "We need to thank you kids for exposing his black market business, even though you shouldn't have been out exploring in the middle of the night."

Ms. Stad shot the Code Busters a look that reminded them they were still in trouble.

"What about the other guy?" Luke asked. "The one from the ferry who was helping him?"

"That would be Felix Farley. Police traced him based on your description. He was arrested too. The police found quite a collection of counterfeit artifacts in his apartment, waiting to be sold to unsuspecting tourists."

The Code Busters grinned at one another.

Matt the Brat came limping up, using a stick to support himself, his ankle wrapped in a bandage. With his hair sticking out like a porcupine's quills, he looked kind of funny wearing superhero pajamas. *Super Porcupine*, Cody thought, and laughed to herself.

"No more sleepwalking last night, Matthew?" Ms. Stad said, raising her famous eyebrow. Cody knew her teacher suspected Matt had lied, but Cody didn't want to embarrass him in front of everyone. The Code Busters had agreed to tell their teachers the truth in private.

"Nope," said Matt. He looked at the box in Mika's hand. "What's that?"

"Mika, where did you get that?" Ms. Stad asked, suddenly noticing the object.

"We found it," Mika answered. "It was hidden in the old kitchen at the immigration station."

Ranger Yee shook her head. "I'm sorry, honey, but if you discovered it on national park property, it belongs to the museum and has to remain here."

"But . . ." Mika's eyes filled with tears. "I think it's my great-great grandfather's. My mother and grandmother told me he used to hide a puzzle box filled with special treasures for my great-great-grandmother while they were on the island. It's the only way they could communicate."

Ms. Stad looked at the ranger. "Ranger Yee, if it did belong to her relative, then I believe it is her property."

Ranger Yee looked concerned. "Well, let's open it and find out what's inside. That may tell us something about the original owners. May I?"

Mika reluctantly handed the box to the ranger, who turned it over in her hand several times, her frown deepening. "Hmm, maybe this doesn't open at all," Ranger Yee said. "There's no lid. No hinges. I think it's just a block of carved wood."

"Let me open it," Matt said, reaching for it.

"No way," Cody said. "You could break it. Let Mika try."

Mika took the box from the ranger and held it for a moment, rubbing her thumbs over the intricately carved wood. She began to gently but firmly press one side of the box, as if trying to slide it open. Nothing happened. She turned the box over and tried again. This time the side of the box slid forward a quarter of an inch.

"Awesome!" M.E. said. "It moved!"

Everyone looked on as Mika continued to work intently, rubbing and pushing the sides of the box.

Mika turned the box over again. "Japanese legends say that if a person can open a Koyosegi puzzle box, he or she will receive good luck." She pushed another side in the opposite direction of the first side. It also moved forward a quarter of an inch.

"That's so cool!" Cody said. "It really *is* a puzzle box. I never would have figured out how to open it."

Mika continued pressing and sliding the sides of the box. One by one, the sides slid out, a little bit each time. She pushed once more, and the top of the box slid completely off.

"Oh my gosh!" M.E. said. "You got it open! So what's inside? Show us!"

Mika carefully handed the lid to Cody. She reached into the small space and pulled out a tiny object wrapped in a ragged piece of faded silk. Peeling the fabric open, she revealed a tarnished silver locket. She held it up, clicked the latch on the locket, and flicked it open with her thumbs.

Mika gasped. "My great-great grandparents," she whispered.

After a moment, she turned the locket so everyone could see. Inside were two yellowed photographs, one on each side. The man in the photo on the left wore a black suit with a round collar. The woman on the right had on a white dress with a high neck.

She pointed to the man. "That's my great-great-grandfather, Hiraku Takeda! Or Senjin, his pen name. And my great-great-grandmother, Yuka. We have an old picture just like this at home, only with them standing together. These two images must be cut from another copy of their wedding picture."

"Awesome," Cody whispered. "The locket's so old and delicate. And the picture is so faded."

"Hiraku left it for Yuka to find," Mika said, "but she never did, so it's been hidden all these years." She closed the locket and noticed a tiny engraving on the back, written in Japanese characters. "It says 'Senjin,' the name he used when he wrote his poems."

"Well, I guess you might be right, Ms. Stadelhofer," Ranger Yee said. "If those really are pictures of her ancestors, the box and the locket belong to this young lady and her family. The inscription seems to confirm it."

"Your family will be so happy you found it," M.E. said, giving Mika a hug.

Mika nodded, her eyes shining.

"Thank you so much for helping me find it," she said to the Code Busters. "I'm so sorry I got you all into trouble." She turned to her teacher. "Ms. Stadelhofer, I'm sorry I broke the rules. It's all my fault."

Ms. Stad was smiling. "Well, Mika, obviously I wish you had told me or a chaperone about this instead of trying to find it on your own. But I understand what this means to you and your family."

"And it all worked out," Cody said. "Not only did we find the box, but we figured out what Schnikey was doing. Even Matt helped in a way."

Ms. Stad frowned. "Yes, but about the sleepwalking . . ."

Matt the Brat cut her off. "Guess what! You know my relative, Vincenzo Gambi? He was one of Jean Lafitte's pirates, you know. Anyway, he used to sleepwalk too. I read that on Wikipedia."

Ms. Stad shook her head, obviously not believing a word of Matt's claim.

Cody had also looked up Vincenzo Gambi and had discovered the Italian pirate was, in the words of one website, a "violent, ruthless, murdering privateer, looting and sinking ships," until he was finally killed by his own men while asleep on a pile of gold he'd kept hidden from his crew. There was no mention of Pirate Gambi sleepwalking.

But Cody kept that information to herself. She felt sorry for Matt, and she appreciated that he wasn't trying to get the Code Busters in trouble anymore. If he wanted to tell everyone his pirate ancestor was a sleepwalker, that was fine. For now.

* * *

When the kids returned to their clubhouse after school on Monday, Mika handed each of the Code Busters a wrapped present the size of a half cube of butter. They opened their gifts and found their own Japanese Koyosegi puzzle boxes.

"How cool!" M.E. squealed, holding hers up. Each box had a different wood-carved pattern. The kids immediately went to work on opening their puzzle boxes. Inside, they each found a rolled-up piece of fabric. Cody unrolled hers and saw it was rectangular with a pointed notch at the top, much like a bookmark.

Running down the front of the fabric, written in black marker, were these letters:

Oyu heav draccek het deco

She frowned at it. "What does it say?" she asked Mika, thinking it might be Japanese—although the characters didn't look Japanese.

Mika only smiled. Cody knew instantly this was some kind of code. The others unrolled their pieces of fabric, but each one had a different set of letters. M.E. showed hers to everyone. It read,

Uyo deepon

Quinn held his up, which read,

teh zepluz xob

And Luke revealed his:

Dogo cluk liwl eb soury.

Code Busters Solution found on p. 180.

"These are anagrams!" said Luke, the expert anagram solver. "We have to decode them."

The kids got out paper and pencils and began working on their individual anagram codes. When they finished putting the letters in the correct order to form familiar words, the message still didn't make any sense.

"That's because we have to figure out the *order* of the message," Cody said, smiling at Mika for creating such a clever puzzle. "Right, Mika?"

Mika nodded.

"Will you give us a hint?" M.E. asked.

"The message is a haiku," Mika answered.

"Ahhh," Cody said. "So the first line has five beats, the second has seven, and the last has five again."

"But there are four parts to the puzzle. That's more than three lines," M.E. said.

Cody spread the four pieces of the message on the floor and studied them. She rearranged the lines by connecting two of them, to make seven beats. Then she read the answer aloud.

"Thanks, Mika!" Cody said, giving her friend a

hug. "That was fun. And I can use this piece of fabric as a bookmark."

"Good idea," Mika said. "It's called an *omamori*. My grandmother taught me how to make them out of silk. They're used for good luck and for protection. Since the Code Busters seem to get into trouble once in a while, I thought maybe we all could use a little more protection."

The Code Busters laughed. It was true, Cody thought. They needed all the good luck and protection they could get. She'd be taking her omamori with her on their next adventure, just in case there was more trouble . . .

Cody's cell phone chirped. Someone was texting her. But all the Code Busters were in the clubhouse, so who could it be? She read the message: *Ges wat! I gt us tkts 2 somplc cool 4 sprng brk!*

"Oh man," Cody said to the others, giggling. "My mom's trying to text me, and she's just randomly shortening all the words!"

Cody texted her back, using her mother's style of leaving out letters and changing words into numbers. *Wht abt the CBs? Cn they come 2?*

Y, if they pay thr own wy, came the reply.

K%l! Cody answered.

Code Busters Solution found on p. 180.

She translated the message from her mother for the others.

"Wow," M.E. said. "When it comes to good luck, this omamori thingy really works!"

"Yeah, but how are we going to get the money to pay for a trip?" Luke said. "My grand-mere doesn't have a lot. She's always watching what she spends."

"I have an idea," Mika said. "I can teach all of you how to make omamori! We could make a bunch of them out of fun fabrics, like superheroes and cartoon characters and codes, and then sell them!"

"Awesome!" Cody said. "Spring break adventures, here we come!"

CODE BUSTERS'

Key Book
&
Solutions

Keys & Solutions

Alphanumeric Code:

1	2	3	4	5	6	7	8	9	10	11	12	13	14	15
A	B	C	D	E	F	G	H	I	J	K	L	M	N	O

16	17	18	19	20	21	22	23	24	25	26
P	Q	R	S	T	U	V	W	X	Y	Z

International Morse Code:

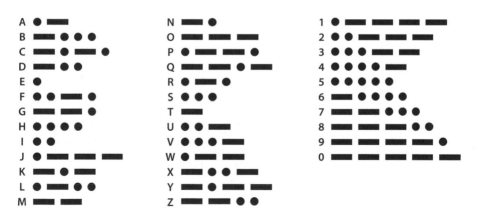

167

International Flag Code:

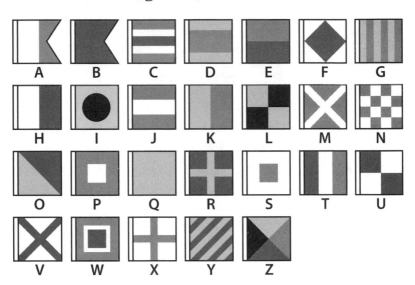

Semaphore Code:

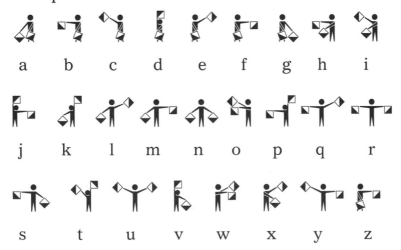

Pigpen Code:

Key Version 1

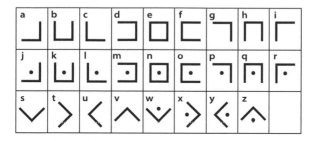

Key Version 2

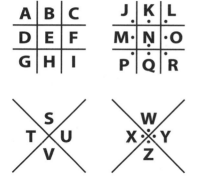

American Indian Symbols:

 HORSE
Journey

 MAN
Human Life

 SUN RAYS
Constancy

 THUNDERBIRD
Sacred Bearer of
Happiness Unlimited

 LASSO
Captivity

 CROSSED ARROWS
Friendship

 ARROW
Protection

 ARROWHEAD
Alertness

 4 AGES
Infancy, Youth,
Middle and Old Age

 CACTUS
Sign of the Desert

 RAIN CLOUDS
Good Prospects

 **LIGHTNING and
LIGHTNING ARROW**
Swiftness

 DAYS AND NIGHTS
Time

 MORNING STARS
Guidance

 SUN SYMBOLS
Happiness

 RUNNING WATER
Constant Life

 RAINDROP-RAIN
Plentiful Crops

 TEEPEE
Temporary Home

 SKY BAND
Leading to Happiness

 MEDICINE MAN'S EYE
Wise, Watchful

 CACTUS FLOWER
Courtship

 SADDLE BAGS
Journey

 BIRD
Carefree, Lighthearted

 LIGHTNING SNAKE

 SNAKE
Defiance, Wisdom

 THUNDERBIRD TRACK
Bright Prospects

 DEER TRACK
Plenty Game

 BEAR TRACK
Good Omen

 RATTLESNAKE JAW
Strength

 HEADDRESS
Ceremonial Dance

 BUTTERFLY
Everlasting Life

 HOGAN
Permanent Home

 BIG MOUNTAIN
Abundance

 HOUSE OF WATER

 FENCE
Guarding Good Luck

 **ENCLOSURE FOR
CEREMONIAL
DANCES**

 EAGLE FEATHERS
Chief

 **WARDING OFF
EVIL SPIRITS**

 PATHS CROSSING

 PEACE

 GILA MONSTER
Sign of the Desert

 COYOTE TRACKS

 MOUNTAIN RANGE

Phonetic Alphabet:

A = Alpha	J = Juliet	S = Sierra
B = Bravo	K = Kilo	T = Tango
C = Charlie	L = Lima	U = Uniform
D = Delta	M = Mike	V = Victor
E = Echo	N = November	W = Whisker
F = Foxtrot	O = Oscar	X = X-ray
G = Golf	P = Papa	Y = Yankee
H = Hotel	Q = Quebec	Z = Zulu
I = India	R = Romeo	

Finger Spelling:

a b c d e f g h

i j k l m n o p q r

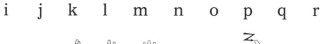

s t u v w x y z

1 2 3 4 5 6 7 8 9

Grid Alphabet

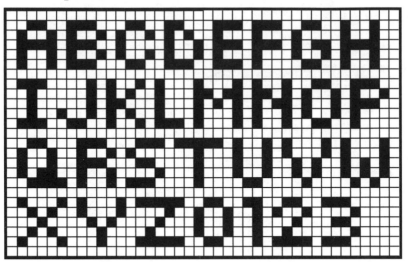

Chapter 1 Solutions

Crossword:

Across

What a detective needs = clue

When something is undiscovered = hidden

6. A black bird = crow

7. What a bird has = wing

8. Electric fish = eels

11. Chew and swallow = eat

13. Outdoor overnight = camping

14. A mighty tree = oak

16. Insects that buzz = bees

18. A palindrome of TOOT = otto

19. Trees have this = root

20. Look for clues = search

21. What we'll be taking = trip

Down

1. What spies use = code

2. Listen with these = ears

3. Who, what, when, where, why, and = how

4. Also called sunrise = dawn

5. When you sleep = nights

6. Use to tell time = clock

9. A tall, fuzzy Australian bird = emu

10. Breathe this = air

11. A tall white bird = egret

12. What a rainbow has = colors

15. See the sites = tour

16. Our ride to our destination = boat

17. The immigrants' ride to their destination = ship

18. Give a cheer! = rah

Anagram: Angel Island

Country codes:

IN – India   •• —•

MX – Mexico   —— —•• —

TH – Thailand   — ••••

AF – Afghanistan   •— ••—•

RU – Russia   •—• ••—

AU – Australia   •— ••—

IE – Ireland   •• •

TR – Turkey   — •—•

PK – Pakistan   •——• —•—

IL – Israel   •• •—••

CN – China   —•—• •—

KE – Kenya   —•— •

JP – Japan   •——— •———•

BR – Brazil   —••• •—•

VN – Vietnam   •••— —•

FR – France   ••—• •—•

IR – Iran   •• •—•

PH – Philippines   •——• ••••

UK – United Kingdom   ••— —•—

CA – Canada   —•—• —•

IT – Italy   •• —

Flag code: Draw and color your ancestral flags.

Chapter 3 Solutions

Morse code: CJ

Flag code: be where of pirites on anjel iland
  (Beware of pirates on Angel Island!)

Chapter 4 Solutions

Semaphore: Set up camp, then meet at the
  visitor's center with your lunch.

Morse code: Meet me at noon at the usual place.

Pigpen code: head to Camp Reynolds

American Indian symbols: bird, running water,
  mountain range animal track, fence

Chapter 5 Solutions

Flag code:

  Take a picture of the Rock,

  Once Al Capone's home,

  The place has gone to the birds.

  (Answer: Alcatraz)

Phonetic alphabet code: Whose motto is "Honor.
  Respect. Devotion to Duty"?

Chapter 6 Solutions

Sign language:

What was Matt doing out there?

I think he was looking for treasure.

Maybe he believes he's a real pirate.

Did you notice how mad Schnikey got?

Yeah. I don't trust that guy. He's been acting really strange.

We should keep an eye on him.

Alphanumeric code:

What's missing? Solv my riddl and tak a pictur. You'll find me

At the beginning of eternity

At the end of time and space

At the beginning of every end,

And at the end of every place.

(Answer: the letter *e)*

Pig Latin: Looks like lots of money.

Semaphore: Let's go!

Finger spelling:

Guys, I think I recognized the man Schnikey was talking to.

Who?

He was on the ferry. He had a tattoo that looked like the Jolly Roger. And I think we saw the signal that Schnikey sent him.

Chapter 7 Solutions

Grid:

Phonetic alphabet code: Let's get out of here!

Chapter 8 Solutions

Finger spelling: I'll bet the gift is hidden in the station's kitchen, behind the stove!

Morse code:

Ready?

Ready!

Meet behind the latrine in five minutes

Ten-four

Be careful

You too!

Finger spelling:

What?

I heard a noise. It came from the stairs.

Chapter 9 Solutions

Semaphore: Stay there! I'll come up and unlock the door!

Morse code: SOS

Chapter 10 Solutions

Finger spelling: Coast is clear. Let's make a run for the golf cart.

Chapter 11 Solutions

Pig Latin: I think we're in big trouble.

Morse code: What's in the box?

Chapter 12 Solutionshh

Anagrams:

You have cracked the code.

You opened the puzzle box.

Good luck will be yours.

Text messages:

Guess what! I got us tickets to someplace cool for spring break!

What about the Code Busters? Can they come too?

Yes, if they pay their own way.

Cool!

For more adventures with the Code Busters Club, go to www.CodeBustersClub.com.

There you'll find:

1. Full dossiers for Cody, Quinn, Luke, and M.E.
2. Their blogs
3. More codes
4. More coded messages to solve
5. Clues to the next book
6. A map of the Code Busters neighborhood, school, and mystery

Suggestions for How Teachers Can Use the Code Busters Club Series in the Classroom

Kids love codes. They will want to "solve" the codes in this novel before looking up the solutions. This means they will be practicing skills that are necessary to their class work in several courses, but in a non-pressured way.

The codes in this book vary in level of difficulty so there is something for students of every ability. The codes move from a simple code wheel—Caesar's Cipher wheel—to more widely accepted "code" languages such as Morse code, semaphore and Braille.

In a mathematics classroom, the codes in this book can easily be used as motivational devices to teach problem-solving and reasoning skills. Both of these have become important elements in the curriculum at all grade levels. The emphasis throughout the book on regarding codes as patterns gives students a great deal of practice in one of the primary strategies of problem solving. The strategy of "Looking for a Pattern" is basic to much of mathematics. The resolving of codes demonstrates how important patterns are. These codes can lead to discussions of the logic behind why they "work," (problem solving). The teacher can then have the students create their own codes (problem formulation) and try sending secret messages to one another, while other students try to "break the code." Developing and resolving these new codes will require a great deal of careful reasoning on the part of the students. The class might also wish to do some practical research in statistics, to determine which letters occur most frequently in the English language. (E, T, A, O, and N are the first five most widely used letters and should appear most often in coded messages.)

This book may also be used in other classroom areas of study such as social studies, with its references to code-breaking machines, American Sign Language, and Braille. This book raises questions such as, "Why would semaphore be important today? Where is it still used?"

In the English classroom, spelling is approached as a "deciphering code." The teacher may also suggest the students do some outside reading. They might read a biography of Samuel Morse or Louis Braille, or even the Sherlock Holmes mystery "The Adventure of the Dancing Men."

This book also refers to modern texting on cell phones and computers as a form of code. Students could explain what the various "code" abbreviations they use mean today and why they are used. —*Dr. Stephen Krulik*

Dr. Stephen Krulik has a distinguished career as a professor of mathematics education. Professor emeritus at Temple University, he received the 2011 Lifetime Achievement Award from the National Council of Teachers of Mathematics.